I0571916

# REX STORIES

## RICK LAWTON

Sasha Press
San Francisco, CA
www.sashapress.com

Published 2012

Published by Sasha Press
San Francisco, CA
www.sashapress.com

ISBN 978-0-9788862-4-0

Library of Congress Control Number: 2011935597

Printed in the United States of America

Your tale, sir, would cure deafness.


Shakespeare
The Tempest

# REX STORIES

# Prelude

Rudi Lopwitz walked quickly down Twenty-eighth Street towards the Rex. Before he got there, he stopped and looked up at it, the same way he had ten years ago. Even then, the building was a throwback, a turn-of-the-century anachronism, a dark fortress with a shade blinking like an eyelid from a top-floor window. Ten years ago, he had walked hesitantly in the door and, in a twist he was still trying to unravel, found himself part-owner, manager, and permanent handyman of the fortress.

Rudi walked by the Moat, the basement bar anchoring the Rex on the west, tapped a Rex pillar three times with a knuckle, then hopped up the shallow steps.

He walked through the open door at exactly six o'clock. Ivan, the night clerk of the week, was up, bleary-eyed, slack-jawed, fixed like an effigy of suffering in the half-oval cutout of the wall of the lobby.

"Problems?" said Rudi.

"Nyet," said Ivan, scratching his ferret-like head.

"Go, go," said Rudi.

Rudi watched Ivan disappear from the window and a few minutes later punch the call button on the elevator. Rudi listened to the grinding of the winch, the creaking cables, the whirring motor. The little red elevator stopped where it was supposed to, and Ivan got in and the elevator ground upwards. Rudi, relieved, walked into a cluttered room made small by an office in back, an ancient switchboard, and a looming honeycomb of mailboxes. Rudi picked a Manhattan phone book out of the office, placed it on the clerk's chair, edged onto the phone book, and took up his position as point man on an excursion into familiar but perilous country.

Rudi Lopwitz was sixty, small, had an egg-shaped head, small tight mouth, abrupt nose, and thick curly salt-and-pepper hair. His short-sleeved shirt hung loose, and the end of his long belt, cinched tight around baggy pants, flopped over his pants like a lolling tongue. He made an unkempt but tough figure in the half-oval. He found a pencil, took a pair of coke-bottle glasses out of a large shirt pocket, and soon his head was tucked at an angle over the cream-colored pages of the Rex ledger, the book that reflected the current destinies of the tenants.

Rudi's glasses swiveled into his hair as the early risers trickled past. Brucie—walleyed, bullet-headed and lazy; Brucie said "retired," but he'd never worked as far as Rudi knew—walked down the Rex steps and took up his take up his post leaning against the west pillar. Ric, the nut-brown paranoid Cuban cab driver, left for an odd-hours shift. Ben the troll, the intellectual, slouched up from the basement, then past Brucie, and slipped past the window to Rudi's right. Ben stopped at the light on the corner, where he watched stoplight cycles as if they coded the daily status of the human condition. Ben, the cranky misanthrope, always crossed on red, and Rudi looked concerned when Ben glanced at the Giltmore, turned, and slouched back to the Rex without trying.

Ben's steel-white bristles edged into the half-oval. Ben looked like a Daumier prune. "Ha...hee, hee." The prune split open, letting out a dry seed of sharp laughter that hung in the lobby after Ben slipped downstairs.

Ben was a premonition. It made Rudi think of the Giltmore. It rose like a phantom across Lexington and from the Olympia. The Giltmore coalesced his fears. It was new, shiny steel and glass, rich, and an omen. Every time he saw its gleaming chrome entrance over his shoulder, he felt vulnerable, exposed, as if the hunched body of Rudi Lopwitz were naked before a leering giant.

Around eight, he had his hands full of tenants. They came in a stream, or tides, some ebbing out, others out and back in. He collected rent, nodded at those he knew well, buzzed the rooms for phone calls, and watched street people and joggers through the window or open door.

He was informed of minor changes in the morning routines. The Farmers, urban equivalent of American Gothic, a study in decaying rectitude, took an early breakfast at the Odyssey, not Plato's, where they'd complained about the service once too often. Matie said he'd forsaken the Persian grocery on First for the new Korean deli on the corner. Sven, the eighth-floor painter of miniatures, told him he was teaching a new class at the Senior Center on Second. Frieda, a stalwart, a descendent of Swiss and Russian Jews, stopped for a fashion consult, but when he mentioned cutting back her illegal garden on the roof, took off like a dervish.

It looked like an easy day—too easy—when he got a crabby phone call from Rose Tutwiler about the toilet on six. Rudi sighed, ripped a blank piece of paper from the back of the ledger, and started the List. The List was annoying, irritating, but curiously reassuring. It let Rudi know the Rex was still there alive and complaining.

The List had grown to two toilets and one window, when Luce Shaw, slim, big brown eyes, hyperactive but with a haunted look, breezed into the lobby, pivoted at the door, and came back to harass him.

"Rudi."

Luce's eyes, sad that morning, saddened him.

"I try to be stoical about living here." The preamble was bad. He knew it wasn't tangible. He knew it wasn't a leaky faucet. The possibilities were numerous—the new guy next to her, Tex, the ragtag bike messengers on three, Gino sleeping at the desk.

Luce shifted a large brown bag to her other shoulder. "I've lived here almost three years—a feat for anyone—and I've managed to live with drafts, zero water pressure, and terminal elevator noise." Luce seemed to reflect as if she wondered why she'd put up with all of that.

"And..."

"And I live on the revolving-door floor. People stay for a day and cop fire extinguishers."

"I caught him, remember."

Luce dismissed his defense with a head-shake. "I now live across the floor from Harry. I don't pry into what Harry does, or did, although I've heard he's a doctor, and I'm curious." Harry seemed solid and paid on time. How an out-of-work doctor had landed in the Rex *was* a mystery.

Luce plunged her hand into her brown bag. It came out empty. "What time is it?"

Rudi looked at the clock. "You'll only be a little late—8:15."

Luce ignored his demure. "This mislaid Hippocrates has started to bug me. He waits for me to go to the bathroom. I open my door, he opens his. I close my door, he closes his. I guess he needs patients—maybe he thinks I'm sick." Luce allowed herself a quick smile. Rudi thought she was going to leave, but she paused, looked at the elevator, and reflected, "I haven't had a friend visit here for months."

"I don't have any friends," said Rudi.

"I'm not competing." Luce brought her big eyes close. Rudi moved back, tucked his glasses securely in his hair. "I'm here for the record. If this keeps up, something is going to happen."

"Harry's OK—we have problems with the bathrooms."

"He's not a stopped-up toilet." Luce turned and hurried out the door. Rudi listened to the fading tapping of her shoes.

Rudi glanced at the fire door through the open door to the desk and wondered if a problem had surfaced from the murky depths of the first floor. The first floor was the transient floor except for Luce and Matie. It was a litmus. If the first floor was OK, the other floors were too. It was too early to tell, and it was a problem he couldn't put on the List.

Rudi liked concrete problems, not vaporous ones. How to fit Harry into the calculation, an algorithm that took rooms, tenants, the physical wounds, the band-aids, and came up with a plus, a minus, or, the more usual shaky balance. There had been an invasion of question marks in the past week: the kid he'd put on six, Rocky, the ex-fighter on seven, Tex, and now the little problem with Harry. Rudi sensed the internal balance shifting, leaning.

Brucie emerged from the elevator, walked through the lobby, his walleyes scanning Rudi from under his reversed Yankees cap. He turned at the front door. "The shower on six, Rudi. Two feet of water. I caught a carp a few minutes ago."

"I'll get it! You might look for a job, Mr. Behind-in-rent!"

Rudi popped his glasses down, scratched a new entry on the List.

Rudi looked at the clock, saw it was nine, and came out from behind the desk and stood in the doorway. Cars, joggers, fast walkers, a couple with tennis racquets. Brucie leaned on the pillar; the voices from early drinkers in the Moat scratched the surface of the morning. Rudi knew his job was to worry about the pluses and minuses, the internal balance, the leaky faucets, the Harrys. But he'd started worrying more about the outside, a threat that escaped the algorithm, that was slowly tilting the stone and bricks of the Rex in a larger calculation.

A door opened and closed. Rudi heard his name, and he turned and saw Gino waiting to take over the desk. It was time to start on the List.

# Luce

Luce Shaw, soaked in sweat, nodded at Ivan and made her way through the fire doors. She glanced suspiciously at the door across the carpet. A few minutes later she threw her bag on the desk and kicked off her shoes. Luce propped herself on her bed, back against the wall. She adjusted her legs on the bed and admired them.

Luce had seen the first floor at its worst. She'd endured heat, drafts, noise, transience, and had become—through comparative youth, fearlessness, and seniority—de facto chief of floor security. Luce extracted a cigarette from her bag, lighted it, tapped it into a glass ashtray, and mulled over two recent additions to the first floor: Tex and Harry. Tex was a pseudo-cowboy with a sloping nose, and eyes like inverted telescopes. He had the room next to her from which she'd heard doggish noises followed by long silences.

Harry was a question mark. She'd never met Harry—officially—but she'd seen him. He was big, possibly Swedish, and she—and everyone else—wanted to know how a doctor had landed in the Rex. But it was more than the mystery that puzzled her; it was what happened when she opened her door at night. She always took a shower at 6:30, and for the last few nights Harry's door opened too close after hers to be coincidence.

Luce uncrossed her legs, stood at her desk, felt the worn rug between her toes, regarded an old photo of Sartre behind the chair, then looked at the dull bricks beyond her window. Shelves of books—a miniature library—crowded her reflection. Luce was slim, had a fine tapered face, and big light brown eyes that attracted people but made them wary at the same time. Sometimes she worried about that, but usually she didn't and was content to sit in her stuffed chair, switch on her tasseled lamp, and lose herself in her books.

Luce looked at her image again, turned away, glanced at the book-shelves in the alcove, then slipped into her red bathrobe and slippers, picked up her shower gear, and after letting a Cubist scarf on the door drift through her fingers, wondered what would happen when she opened her door.

Luce balanced a white towel that said "The Palace," a bar of Dove in a soap dish, and Nexxus shampoo as she peeked through the crack to see if anyone was in the good can. The door was open and the light off, so she slipped through and locked her door. She was halfway to the can when Harry's door creaked open. Luce tightened her robe around her and hurried towards the can. As she rounded the opaque windows of the phone room, the Nexxus slipped and when she grabbed it, the Dove escaped from the soap dish, bounced once, and lay on the carpet like a newly laid egg. Cursing, Luce picked up the soap and hurried through the open door of the bathroom, closed, and locked it.

Luce looked at the door, heard a flat whistle and a heavy tread, and tipped herself over the line. "Pervert!"

Luce heard the whistling stop, a door close. It was hot, and Luce wondered why she did it; better to smell a little than play games, pretend one is getting clean, and sweat anyway. Luce picked up and dropped a soap wrapper into the wastebasket. She flipped the toilet lid down, arranged the towel, soap, and shampoo on it, and took off her robe.


Luce had decided to spend the night with her books, but her skirmish with Harry had ruined her concentration. She checked the *Times* and saw the Museum of Modern Art was open late. Half an hour later, she strolled through the museum's first-floor sculpture garden—the Matisse backs looked like an intriguing exercise, the Picasso goat hideous but strangely alluring. Then she took in a photo exhibit of tricky, soulless cityscapes that left her feeling flat empty. After an hour, she left and walked to the West Side and took a subway to her favorite bar in Chelsea, the Misty. She was told she just missed Maritsa, therapist and confidante, and it was mid-week slow. After half an hour, she left and walked back to the Rex.

Luce closed her door, turned on her lamp, and scanned the French section of her shadowed library, tapping on the mauve covers, finally picking Alphonse Daudet, the French Dickens, hoping she'd be swept into the insular, bucolic world of a windmill in Provence.

When that didn't work, she'd tried *The Pickwick Papers* but soon put it down next to her reading light, unread. She watched the crossed edges of scarves on the door and listened to the sounds of the Rex—the elevator, voices from the lobby, the shower, and a clacking sound like a wind chime.

At eleven, there was a feeble tapping on her door, and a thin, hesitant voice.

Luce palmed her Mace and a few seconds later regarded Matie, the seventy-five-year-old retired carpenter who lived at the end of the hall. They shared a look that conjured exhibits in the Hallway of Horrors. Matie pointed to Tex's door.

*Clack, clack, clack.*

They both listened, and Luce stepped into the hall and looked next door. She saw Tex from the thin rectangle of the cracked door, sitting on his heels, his long hair hiding his face.

Beyond Tex, a shade hit the window frame.

*Clack, clack, clack.*

Matie shrugged and looked at her. Luce whispered, "I'll take care of it." She knew that was what Matie wanted to hear. Matie turned, paused at Tex's door, and rubbed his bald head, as if the noise had stirred a remote memory.

*Clack, clack...clack, clack.*

Luce considered her options: 911, police, and regardless of what happened, a strident attack on Rudi in the morning. She decided to wait and see if Tex pulled out of it. She closed her door and wondered why smack freaks did that—sat on their heels. She'd seen them in the Bowery, squatting on their heels, crotch protected by their arms and head. Tex's arms looked leaden, his head pulled down by a stone around his neck, hidden in a veil of black hair. Frieda, Rex gardener and welfare worker, told her smack freaks were like flies crawling the sides of smooth-walled carnivorous plants. They saw light around the lip, felt a sandpaper grittiness, but then the sandpaper eroded, the light faded, and they slipped down, down, down.

Luce checked on Tex at midnight. The narrow light from the hall crossed a jumble of cowboy boots, a Budweiser buckle, and hair that spread on the rug like a black mop. Luce reflected, shrugged, and walked into the lobby where she helped Ivan call 911. A few minutes later, she watched Tex being strapped to a stretcher, pupils like pinholes.

After they carried Tex away, Luce watched the police check the room and confiscate the rig. Then Luce helped Ivan with the questions and finally, after one, headed back to her room. She was about to close the door when Harry walked past the opaque glass window of the phone room.

Luce watched him for a second, her eyes hardened, and her anger spilled out. She strode across the floor and came up to Harry. "I've had enough weird shit."

Harry stared at her curiously. "The police—"

"Don't change the subject."

"What is the subject?"

"Lurking, watching me, slapstick with doors."

Luce watched Harry frown, then laugh. "I'm too big to lurk."

Luce eyed Harry suspiciously. "Don't be friendly."

"I'm a man who wants to take a shower. I usually take them in the morning, but I couldn't the last week—early interviews."

Doubt seeded itself, grew, cracked her certainty. "You're saying it was bad timing."

"I can see why you might be paranoid."

Luce thought of the doors, the opening and closing, and saw that First Floor Paranoia had spun her around and pointed her in the wrong direction.

Harry was solid, weighed about two-twenty, was about six-two. She'd screamed at him, called him names. Luce shrugged inwardly. "There's been an epidemic of ambulances. This time it was Marlboro-man. Rudi will hear about it tomorrow, believe me." Luce looked at Harry closer; he was concerned, unflappable. He had the Doctor Aura.

"He's been pestering me for days...for drugs." Harry paused. "If I bother you, I'll go back to mornings. I'll wake up earlier."

"Don't do that. I have nerve endings in the rooms. I get too sensitive." Luce knew she was tired, but she watched Harry, wondering, again, what he was doing in the Rex.

"I don't know how you sleep with all the noise. I got these today." Harry produced a bottle of pills and stifled a yawn. "Sleeping pills."

Luce looked at the bottle then Harry's face and was struck by his solidity.

"I may have to try something myself."

"Want some? Dime a dozen."

Luce shook her head. "No thanks."

14

Matie's door opened down the hall, and he looked out.

Luce indicated Tex's door with her head, and Matie nodded and closed his door.

"Wait a second." Harry opened his door, and Luce saw books in boxes, framed diplomas on the desk, and an open suitcase in the closet, the whole giving the impression of a man between realities who expected his current resting place to be, at most, brief. Harry came back with an empty bottle into which he poured some pills.

Luce took the bottle, looked into Harry's face and forced a smile. "Why not?" Harry smiled back and that made her feel better. "Sorry I called you names."

Back in her room, Luce lit a cigarette and wondered about the stupid mistake with Harry. She'd been feeling strange lately, as if she were irritated at something, at herself, life. She'd begun to feel she'd warped into a rare phase where she couldn't think about the future. She told Maritsa that she felt like a bug mounted on a dirty satin board, who was happy right there. At least on the board, you knew where you were .

That's why everyone stays, she decided, as she curled up in her large chair, then fingered the slick cover of *Lettres de mon Moulin*; at least you know where you are.

\* \* \*

Rudi looked over his glasses and stopped Luce with his palm. "You got mail."

Luce had a note in her box, which made her suspicious. She read it as she transferred her bag from her right to her left shoulder. It was from Harry asking if she'd slept better.

"Rudi, ring Harry's room for me."

"He left early—job interview in Queens."

"I can't talk anyway." She pulled open her bag, and after turning over a brown checkbook, change purse, matches, and a business card, found a chewed-up pen and a notebook. She thought for a second, then scribbled a few words, line angling forward as if the words were going to fly off the page, tore out the sheet and gave it to Rudi. "Put it in Harry's box."

"Yesterday you wanted Harry assassinated; today you leave little notes."

"Everyone makes a mistake." Luce smiled, added a twist, leaned into the half-oval. "Say, Rudi, what happened to screening, or was that cowboy a test?"

Rudi touched his glasses, and his eyes flipped back and forth as if he were looking for a place to hide. "I do my best, but if somebody has money."

Luce shook her head. "The same lame bottom-line excuse. Use your imagination."

"I knew he was trouble." Rudi sighed. "I hope it's not a trend. I got a bad feeling."

"You always have a bad feeling. Gotta go."

Later that evening, Luce listened, peeked out the door, and a few seconds later walked slowly towards the good bathroom with her Nexxus, soap dish, and towel. She half-expected Harry's door to open, but it didn't. Once inside the bathroom, she listened for him but heard the drum of traffic from the street and elevator gears clicking on and off like a loud switch.

She was vaguely disappointed.

Later, she read *Lettres de Mon Moulin* while she listened to Matie scrape by like he was cleaning fish, the showers, the elevator. Finally, she heard a heavy tread on the carpet and knew it wasn't Carrie or her kid Jason. Tex was in Bellevue and would never return. It had to be Harry. She watched her scarves and heard a knock on her door.

She looked at her library, and with a tag-end of self-doubt, put down her book and a few seconds later regarded Harry. He wore a light sports coat and white shirt and reminded her of sausage-fingered gods struggling out of stone in a Swedish museum.

Luce smiled. "Thanks for the pills. I'll try them again—not that I want to get hooked."

Chest hair poked out of his open shirt.

"You live in a library," said Harry.

"I got the gene from Dad."

Harry scanned the titles near the door. "You read German, French?"

"And English. My books, my room, my life. Sometimes I feel I'm

16

in a sanctum sanctorum, sometimes a prison. Did you mean the thing about dinner in your note?"

Harry had a tight sincere smile. "Hungry?"

"Famished."

"So am I. Give me a minute." Luce picked up her purse and closed her door. While Harry rummaged in his room, she wondered what she was doing and whether she was unconsciously starting something she wanted.

They went to Nopalito, a small Italian restaurant a couple of blocks up Second Avenue.

Luce was nervous, at a loss for a topic. Finally she said, "Gino used to work here as a waiter. He got fired for throwing food at yuppies."

"The front desk clerk?" Harry played with his knife and looked at her expectantly.

"I guess you haven't been at the Rex long enough. Gino's an old timer—ten years. You get pens and medals, like working for the same company. I almost classify, myself."

Harry's eyes crinkled, showing nets in the corners. He fell into the conversational swing. "Have you gotten anything?"

"An option on the good bathroom—if it's not being used. This was a neighborhood place—Italians from the Village and Queens came here on the weekend. You can tell it's changing. The latest high-rise was finished last year, and the Olympia is a year old. Besides spawning a flock of sterile expensive eateries, they've invaded our old, good places." Flickering triangles of light highlighted men and women in Armani suits. Some sorted papers, ties and buttons loosened, and tried to read in the weak glow.

"They multiply like fruit flies but don't reproduce."

Luce laughed and wondered about Harry. She'd thought he was a kind of fallen yuppie himself. "Everyone has a little yuppie in them— one day it'll be the new ethic."

"The no-ethics ethic."

"Sometimes, in a romantic mood, I think the Rex is the last refuge of the Real People—that's a rare mood; mostly it's a less-than-creative anachronism. Luce looked at Harry's face, picking out a mole on his cheek, a hint of silver in the curls. "How did the interview go?"

Harry paused, locked his fingers over a barrel chest, and watched the candle.

"By the book. Cordial."

"Job-hunting in New York is the pits."

Harry shrugged, stared at the flame. "I thought it would take a day."

"Keep at it; something will happen."

"I know it will." Harry's face bunched up in an attempt at apology. "I don't suppose you want to endure the saga of Dr. Hamilton."

Luce shrugged. "I like to hear about other people. I get too wrapped up in myself."

Harry looked back at the flame. "Sometimes I wonder what people think of me."

"The Rex grapevine is fast but never gets it right."

A prissy waiter brought salads. Luce picked up her fork, then put it down. "People are curious, including me."

Harry hesitated, sipped his wine. "The fall of Harry was a remarkable example of self-sabotage, of altruism plus small-town naïveté."

"The city has a corner on destroying illusions."

Harry reflected. "I was dedicated, a gadfly. I crusaded against procedures. I tried to improve indigent care. One day I realized I was using OR drugs." Harry paused, thought. "It was the strangest moment of my life: I looked back at the years in medical school, my parents' sacrifices, the long nights, the righteous crusade, and the result was a vial of morphine. Bizarre." Harry ran his hand through his hair, leaving the curls raised, tangled. "I'm not sure I was addicted, but I voluntarily took the cure. When I came back, the board dropped my contract."

Luce regarded Harry's face, curly hair, thick fingers, saw a flicker of incomprehension. "The big question is why you started."

Harry looked into space, as if he'd asked himself the same question and hadn't found an answer. "I don't know—exhaustion, curiosity. I've decided to call it a stupid mistake."

The main course arrived, and they stared at salads, steaming plates of lasagna and pesto. They stared at each other through wisps of steam, not touching the food.

Luce swirled Chianti in her glass and took a sip. "It must be tough not practicing."

Harry shook his head. "It's suspended animation."

"I know about holding patterns."

"I was surprised to find you here."

Luce looked mischievous. "You mean at the Rex?" Luce felt a moment of exhaustion, as if the Luce story were boring, old, but produced a fresh sense of wonder each time she told it. It was like talking about a distant acquaintance. "I'm from Michigan. I lived in Europe for years, mostly Paris—an ESL teacher for hire. I also tried to write, but it was too maudlin, too self-absorbed. When I came back I got married, then a few years later divorced. I came to the Rex three years ago after the divorce. It's been temporary for a long time. Usually, I don't care; I close the door, turn on the light and escape into Provence, the Nevsky Prospekt with Raskolnikov, or shadow Pickwick in the Old Bailey with the other debtors."

"Do you ever think of leaving?"

"New York?" Luce thought. "I have the usual love-hate romance with the city."

Harry paused and said, "Do you mind if I say something?"

"Shoot."

"Has anyone told you you look like Maria Callas?"

Luce laughed. "The old Callas line. My mother's Greek, but let's get serious. We can't let all this food go to waste."

Harry started on his lasagna, and Luce finished her salad. She played with her pesto linguini, watching Harry over the checkered tablecloth as if he were an exotic animal caged by mistake at the Rex. She wasn't surprised when he finished her pasta. She was attracted to Harry, and she reminded herself to control her eyes. Phyllis at *Kids World* told her that when she was nervous, her tiger's eyes started flying in different directions.

Luce was perplexed when she turned on her reading light. She had something new to think about besides the damned struggles of Luce-the-bug. She wove a story around Harry, his big form, curly hair. He was a Swedish bear who'd made a mistake, who liked food too much. It was likely a simple matter of compensation. She knew she should be more careful. She knew there was a desperate quality behind the books, the occasionally bitchy rationalism, her long dance with fate. She shared a tendency with her father to remark the passing world then withdraw.

She knew it made her an easy mark for the few men who drew her out of her sanctuary.

* * *

Luce began thinking of Harry as a pleasant distraction. They talked in the hallway, staggered their showers so they could both use the good bathroom, and life seemed to be back on a normal track. Rudi rented Tex's room to Ralph, a pony-tailed Vietnam vet, a definite improvement over Tex, despite being a cab driver and making wake-up sounds at four in the morning.

The first floor stabilized. Luce's security sensors lowered to near normal. Luce read, battled the Midtown crowds on her way to work, and flipped through the kids' stories. But Harry's struggle made her feel more acutely irritation at her own.

Then Harry left her a note asking her out Thursday. Luce reflected, looked quizzically at her image in the mirror, shrugged, and gave up Alphonse Daudet for Central Park. After work, she walked up Madison and joined Harry at Fifty-ninth Street. They took a quiet walk past the Zoo, Sheep Meadow, and through the artificial glades of the Ramble, where men casually stalked each other, and bird watchers thumbed field guides. Finally, they walked down the steps at Delacorte Castle and joined a fairy ring on the Big Lawn waiting for free tickets for Shakespeare in the Park's *The Merry Wives of Windsor*.

Picnickers ringed the green-brown field. Luce and Harry nibbled on French bread and cheese that Harry produced from his pack.

"I liked the walk. You need people to force you to do things." Luce paused, looked at Harry. "I didn't see you yesterday. Got a job?"

Harry's forehead bunched in a frown. "Almost worked in a small hospital, declined a job in a nursing home."

"A near hit and a near miss?"

"The reference from Kings County has been a problem."

"You should do something about it."

"I've talked to them. I may sue, but I hate lawyers. How are you doing?"

"Up and down. Lately down."

They were both distracted as two small boys fell near their patch of grass and chased each other through the ring, playing tag. Nannies pushed babies around the field, and tourists emerged from the underpass to the Metropolitan with bags of calendars, cards, and books.

Harry watched her. "Why?"

"When I was younger, I worried about the big exciting questions. Now I do local stuff: the Adjustment, escaping, feeling like the bug." Luce watched an actor dressed as Harlequin doing a medley of soliloquies on a portable stage. He was ringed by amused young faces. A red-tailed hawk glided in circles high over the field.

Harry looked at her, amused. "Bug?"

Luce nibbled on a breadstick. "My latest metamorphosis; and no, it's not Kafka's. It's a desultory image I have of myself. I have to quit thinking out loud."

Harry shook his head. "You're young, smart, and a Maria Callas look-alike—what else could you want?"

Luce laughed. "That Callas line will not go away! I don't know, Harry, I go to work, function, do normal things, but the raison d'être is missing. It's been missing for a long time."

Harry shook his head. "You're re-grouping."

"A true Midwestern optimist." Luce looked at her bare legs and sandals; ants filed into an anthill a few feet away.

Harry threw out a crust, and black-bibbed house sparrows flew down and fought over it. "It is hard to think about the future. I usually think about the past and missed options—specializing, sinecures in rich suburbs—or the self-destructive Dr. Hamilton."

"'Self-destructive?' I'm old-fashioned; I go for the throat—guilt, personal responsibility."

"Any explanation will do, as long as you believe it. I haven't found one I believe. I think of my career, then the morphine, and it doesn't add up."

They started giving out tickets. The fairy ring came sluggishly to life. People closed picnic baskets and threw away bottles Luce picked a handkerchief out of her bag, dabbed at beads of sweat on her neck. She said, "I understand what you're doing, but those 'why' questions are unanswerable. Do you know Ben?"

"Who?"

"You've seen him. He's a prune in a trench coat—cynical, unrepentant."

"I've seen him at the stop light."

"He asked too many 'why' questions and became a world-class cynic and pessimist."

Harry chuckled. "Is that a warning or a goal?"

Luce shook her head, laughed. "Harry, we need some comic relief—Falstaff, for example. You know, he gets everything he deserves, but I always feel sorry for him."

"I'll take the side of the women."

"Ah, men and women, the perfect antagonism."

Luce felt her irritation eroding, crumbling. It was dusk, warm, and they picked up their tickets, filed into the theatre, read the programs, adjusted to the hard seats, and saw Falstaff stride across the stage, an aged jokester turned target.

They laughed, lost themselves in the crowd, the bowl of the night. But later it cooled and they huddled close together. Harry sensed she was cold and put his jacket around her, then later, his arm. Luce wondered about that, thought it curious, but left it there as a test. It was a late night, and Luce felt the bug squirming on the satin.

\* \* \*

Luce didn't know what to do with Harry; she'd let herself go, a little, and he'd upset the rhythm, the balance, her interest in a windmill in Provence.

She flipped through an ms at *Kids World*, read a few lines, stopped, and worried about Harry's mistake, then wondered about his mysterious male presence and whether he should be a friend, neighbor, catalyst, or...

She talked to Phyllis about a layout, wide-eyed characters on stylized landscapes, and saw the spine of her secret Album in the shadows. She sighed, stacked books on her desk, and threw herself into a new project hoping to keep the Album shut.

It was hopeless.

The Album flipped by like flash cards, past the yellowed photos of growing up in Illinois of her high-intensity father, poor neglected mother, her straight sisters Peg and Josie. She ticked off high points in Europe, trying to ignore, but homing in as she knew she would on her trip from Paris to Stockholm, and seeing her father the last time. It was a cloud-strewn sky; sinewy girls rolled cigarettes in the café. Her father was an incorrigible German, a successful publisher of three newspapers, lean, almost cadaverous. They'd always had a secret liaison, a secret bond, and he'd asked her to meet him in Stockholm, one of his favorite cities. Cancer perched on his shoulder like a Goya monster, but while they revisited their favorite books, museums, and art for the last time, she began to wonder if her father's real gift to her wasn't books, intelligence, and scruples, but an atavistic germ of despair, a fatalism he'd passed to her like a baton in a long psychic race.

Luce walked down Second Avenue after work, clothes sticking to her, bag biting into her shoulder and tried to trace that fatalism through her father's death, her return from Europe, marriage and divorce. There was the free fall and the Rex. She'd flirted with advertising, editing, and ultimately found a slot at *Kids World*. It was an irony which didn't escape her. Through it all she wondered if below the surface of life, love, laughing, babies, the garish colors of life, was her father's ice-blue conviction that humanity had entered a terminal stage of immense self-delusion. The Album always left her sighing, pining after her own youthful golden age before she ate the fruit of knowledge. It was as if she had that one chance. For the rest, her father had condemned her to be an in absentia monitor of the Adjustment, an extrinsic thing, a slow retreat marred by the occasional skirmish, or man dropping into her life like a deus ex machina.

She said hello to Brucie, rested her back against the pillar, and became a counterpoint gargoyle at the steps into the Rex. She listened to Rudi through the open window, said hello to Ric going in and Mario going out. Soon the hot air rose from the street and encircled her like a wraith. Her blouse stuck to her skin. She admired the shining new marble of the Olympia and felt anger at the Giltmore, all modernistic steel and window, artless and barren. The glossy cars streamed by, and she heard early evening sounds from the bar next to the Rex and thought of her father. Then she thought of Harry and wondered if he was destined to become a shadow in the room.

Luce reluctantly declined Harry's note about dinner and called Maritsa.

At five, she walked onto Frieda's roof garden swinging a just-opened bottle of Chardonnay, clutching two wine glasses in her left hand and throwing rhomboids of light into leaves and flowers. She walked on the flats past the main part of the garden and past the water tower to the far edge.

Water towers poked the skyline towards Twenty-third, but except for the Olympia and the Giltmore, everything was two or three stories, slightly blocked by the feathery leaves of two tall ailanthus trees full of finches, sparrows, and jays. Through the leaves, she glimpsed manicured decks, dogs, a couple entertaining, an older woman playing with a cat in a garden.

Luce sat at a table hidden behind the water tower and poured a glass of Chardonnay. A few minutes later, the scrape of someone on the flats interrupted the buzz of East Side street traffic.

Maritsa sat down.

"Man it's hot. You must be serious." Maritsa shook her head and threw down her bag.

"Thanks for coming. Glass?" Maritsa nodded and Luce poured her a glass.

Maritsa pulled her blouse over her shoulders revealing a deep cleavage. "Every time I see this garden it changes, or maybe it just gets bigger. I don't see how Frieda does it."

"She's tough, the spirit of Old New York. Maritsa, I'm imploding, the Album's a land mine, the Adjustment sucks, I'm starting to feel more like Kafka's bug."

"This is going to take a while."

Luce sighed. "I'll settle for a little devil's advocate."

"A satanic hors d'oeuvres."

Luce felt the heat and unbuttoned the second button on her blouse. "A guy lives across the carpet."

Maritsa took off her sandals and propped her crossed legs on the table. "Sounds bad."

"How bad? I haven't said anything yet."

"Too close. Have him move, then get involved. What happens when you get tired of each other, and you have to stare at each other when you go to the can?"

Luce mused, drank, watched Maritsa pull out a cigarette. "I thought of that. But I think he wants to leave. He's in limbo, bags packed."

"That's good...or bad. Depends if you want a fling."

"I thought of that."

"Why do you need me if you've thought of this stuff?" Maritsa looked at Luce, frowned, uncrossed her legs, seemed to wonder if they were too heavy. "But there is a real problem."

"Yes."

"The balance—that thing we complain about."

"The Adjustment, the balance. That's the real problem."

"He'll cause you grief. I wish he never existed for your sake."

"Now you sound maternal."

"You want another shadow in the room?"

Luce tipped the glass and drank the last few drops. "Shadows. I thought of that."

Maritsa sighed and took a healthy gulp of wine.

Luce said, "How does that shit happen? Should I get out, get married, get back? Why was Dad so gloomy? Why am I damned?"

"This is going to be expensive."

"I'm giving in; I can feel it."

Maritsa said, "Luce, I'm Cassandra. I tell my clients and my friends not to do, and they do. But you know, I think they'd be more fucked up if I weren't here."

"It boils down to boredom, life, and the biological imperative."

"Tough to argue with biology."

The night got cooler; the sky faded to gray. Luce swirled her wine and wondered what to do about Harry.

* * *

25

They had a picnic in her room. Harry sat under Sartre in her big chair and she sat at the desk. Her books crowded them, a layer of uneven insulation. She felt distant, wondering what she was doing, feeling she needed spice, something to get her moving. She looked at Harry and realized, finally, that behind the tough front, she'd gotten lonely. It wouldn't have made any difference if he were Bluebeard.

They ate, drank, talked. Harry laughed at her jokes, always a bad sign, and she found herself caressing him with her eyes. Finally, it was time for Harry to go, and she asked him to stay. She needed the spice—she'd told herself that for months—but hadn't realized she meant it. Harry smiled, but she was stern, tough, serious. She told him that he couldn't stay all night, that he'd have to leave, afterwards. She tried to get the ground rules out as if she weren't asking him, as if she were agreeing to loaning a deck chair.

She turned out the lights. His bulk hid Sartre, obliterated Pickwick. Provence disappeared in a huge dark shadow. She heard a wine glass hit the floor, a plate turn over. The rush of the flesh.

Bed was a tangle; she'd forgotten the minuets, the clumsiness of legs and feet. Gray light poured in from her brick wall and outlined a huge presence hovering over her.

Belly-button alert! He had an outer, a gum-drop.

She wondered what she was doing to her perfect isolation, her Adjustment.

Primeval shapes lunged in the dark, another plate hit the floor...love-making was always like that...wine spilling, food thrown willy-nilly, a tempest that scatters everything in its path. He had thick bones, and beyond the patches of curly hair, smooth sleek skin...she tried to hold herself together, but found herself melting.

Harry was surprisingly deft—like the big man who plays pool like a pro—like Jackie Gleason. God she cried when he died—she really liked Jackie. He always played himself.

How sweet it is!

That touch, that sensitivity at the end of his fingers when he probed her body, when he caressed her hair. Even his sex was like that, deft, like a finger making sure everything was in place, making sure everything was in order.

26

She pictured them in her mind—Maria Callas and pendulous Harry. But it wasn't like that. He had Jackie's touch.

* * *

Luce came home, clothes soaked, slipping off her back in ninety-degree heat. Rudi was about to leave to catch the Number 6 at Twenty-eighth Street.

Rudi glanced at her and said, "Two policemen arrested Harry this afternoon."

Her heart sank. "What? Why?"

"Something about drugs. I called. I tried to find out more."

"As if life isn't hard enough. Hard to fucking believe. Can we do anything?"

"I don't know. Maybe tomorrow."

Luce was detached, but what had happened was sinking in. There was the drawn-out decision, the leap, a light shone in her life, then nothing, almost as if fate had caught her and fixed her back in the Adjustment. "This is fucked up."

Rudi looked at her. "I know, I know." Rudi shook his head, as if he'd had enough worries.

"He didn't do anything! Of course, nothing's fair."

"You perhaps have some dramatic interest in this person?" Rudi swung his glasses up and looked at Luce. "We should have rules about getting too familiar—it complicates things."

"Don't give me a hard time. Where did they take him?"

Rudi sighed, looked at the clock. "Not tonight—you'll confuse things."

"I have to do something!"

"Go to sleep; we'll meddle tomorrow. I can get away at noon."

Luce shook her head. "Sleep?"

Luce changed into her after-work clothes, stuffed money in her jeans, and stayed away from her room as long as she could. She went to the main library at Forty-second Street and walked through its marbled cathedral halls, glancing at horror-filled Kollwitz prints and thinking of Harry in jail. Then she walked Thirty-fourth Street for two hours, a fast walk, like she was going to work, a walk that saw people as animate obstacles: things to deal with, go around, wait for, avoid.

She knew she had to go back.

It wasn't a good night—you don't go from Jackie to nothing that fast. It wasn't a permanent thing, a little fling to keep from getting rusty.

She measured the distance to his door with her eyes and listened to a voice droning from the opaque light in the phone room. Harry's door was stone quiet.

She took her shower late. No crack in the door.

The steam from the shower made the bathroom a sauna; the mirror steamed over. When she opened the door, the steam wisped out, and her robe stuck to her. She hurried to her room.

Luce sat in her big chair, crossed her wet legs on the bed, and stared at the bulb and its shade hanging from the ceiling. She never looked at that light. The Album popped out, and her life strung around the bottom of that bulb, all forty-odd years lined up like a relay. She regressed to a town in Michigan. No she didn't want to get married and have a billion kids and play wifely games. She was the professor's pet, the one who was different, the idealist, the rebel, the peripatetic, the inheritor of her father's real gift, finally, the gloomy adjuster.

But now and then, when the moon was full, she wanted a little of what her sisters had. Somebody like Harry for a few days.

Luce turned the light off. Thin gray light seeped past the brick into the room.

She listened to the elevator as if to an old friend. Feet slipped over the carpet, a distant yell. She listened for Harry's heavy feet, a sound she'd memorized, heavy, dependable, but instead heard the whispering slippers of Matie going to the bathroom.

She reached for the sleeping pills at three in the morning.

# Ric

It was a lead-hot day in August in Manhattan. The top floors of the Rex baked. When Frieda came home via asphyxiating subway from the welfare office in Brooklyn, she stayed less than two minutes in her room and quickly hiked up the stairs to the roof where she potted, repotted, fertilized and soaked her babies, her herb garden and slips with slabs of flowers.

The middle floors of the Rex were cooler, windows open, doors cracked. But everybody worried about something...as far as the residents were concerned, that summer if it wasn't the heat, it was something else.

The couple in 311—the Farmers, John and Melissa—had just opened their door when they found a tiny brown body, upended, legs wiggling on the worn carpet.

"Time for the exterminator," said John.

"Your memory—you poor dear. We've never had an exterminator on this floor."

John was a man in his late sixties with a long face, tired gray eyes flanked by bushy gray eyebrows. His wife told him he looked like John Carradine—the actor—when she was in a good mood. "I didn't mean that we'd had one before," John said irritably. "I wonder if anyone else has them. There's that Cuban boy." John tore off a sheet of toilet paper from a stash near the door and, bending over with difficulty, crushed the roach in the paper between his thumb and index finger.

Melissa was tall for a woman, but shorter than her husband and had a sharp pointed nose and a long narrow face. She had a prayer book in her right hand. They were on their way to the Methodist church on Second Avenue.

"He's not much of a boy anymore. He must be over fifty," she said.

"It's a manner of speaking, Melissa."

"We need some more of that nice Gallo we had last week—the burgundy. You know they have a special at Key Liquors."

"You've only told me a hundred times."

The door to 306 opened and Bill Randall, the Rex handyman, looked out. The length of toilet paper drooped down John's hand like a flat tail. John held up the toilet paper. "Bugs."

Bill was short with a barrel chest, thin legs, and a ponytail. He usually wore his tool belt, but that morning, he was still waking up and his work shirt was out. He shook his head and said, "Last night I saw one scramble across the floor like he was in a track meet." He nodded at the door two down from his. "It's those bike messengers. They have a garbage bag on their floor full of chicken bones, pizza crusts, and Coke cans!"

The Farmers' next-door neighbor, Wayne Holt, a bullet-headed city bus driver, opened his door. The single rooms in the Rex were small, no more than twelve by twelve, and it was hard to keep secrets from your neighbors. Wayne said, "I found one wedged in the lining of my refrigerator. It looked like he was going for my butter brickle."

"I'm going to see Rudi in an hour," said Bill. "I'll tell him."

They shook their heads collectively, and a few minutes later, Wayne closed his door and so did Bill. John leaned in the common bathroom on that side, flipped the paper into the toilet, and flushed it. The paper swirled, and the roach detached itself. The roach was still alive and struggled in the bowl as the water swirled closer and closer to the brown stain until it was sucked into the plumbing.

John pushed open the fire door, and when he saw Melissa waiting for the red elevator, he thought of the resiliency of bugs. One day, he was sure, they would take over the planet.

* * *

Ricardo Montes, Ric the Cuban, parked the cab in a tow-away zone and ran in to check his note in the Times Square pay toilet under the Chock full o'Nuts. He'd left the note on his way to Grand Central an hour before. The note was on a piece of German toilet paper, the brown kind that feels like emery board, and read "he who laughs last, lasts least," encoded in five-letter code groups of his own devising.

It was gone.

Ric was thinking about how long they'd been after him, when, annoyed, he brushed himself with a movement similar to the movement made by Australians in mosquito season, a movement known as the Australian salute. What, he stopped himself, was he brushing off? A large roach scuttled around the corner.

Ah.

Ric contemplated this significant fact. Wasn't it just last week that he'd discovered the first of what was to be an invasion of roaches in his room? Hadn't their population skyrocketed in the last week, and wasn't his room, his spartan room, floor buffed to perfection, now the lieu of those motels where, supposedly, roaches checked in—in twos and threes, on spindly legs, heavy with eggs or under-fridge grime—but not out?

Ric thought about this latest incident of the roach and the Australian salute and its exact connection to the missing German toilet paper and which team of CIA experts was pouring over his latest offering as he raced out of the Chock full o'Nuts.

At the cab, Ric stopped, frozen. Eric, Eric from the Rex, the writer, walked nonchalantly down the other side of Forty-second Street.

Eric seemed like perfect CIA material with that blond hair, blue eyes, and that husky animal build, but there was something about Eric that was out-of-whack, which made him either a perfect CIA reject or a perfect agent. That was the kind of identity of opposites which Ric had read was what primitive gods were about, where the deity contained within itself both positive and negative characters, both good and evil, both rapture and decadence. Not that he thought those things of Eric.

Ric cruised down Forty-third then back up Forty-second and stopped to watch Eric. Eric was watching someone else, who was, probably, watching someone else in turn. Wouldn't it be a gas, Ric thought, if everybody was watching each other in a circle, that everybody needed a conspiracy or plot, because if they didn't the circle would be broken, just like the C&W song. Of course, there was more than one circle. How would one get from circle Y, say, to circle X, if every circle was truly unbroken?

Whatever. He knew one thing: Eric was in a circle, although Ric wasn't precisely sure whether it was the CIA circle or another one. He knew that Eric was not what he said he was. He was hiding his true identity, his reason for living in the Rex. If nothing else, he was a mystery. A mystery similar, Ric reasoned, to the mystery of the CIA, to the mystery of why they'd followed him all those years, to the mystery of the roaches, perhaps the mystery of life, of all those people spying on each other in that big circle.

In Ric's mind, by an alchemy he declined to explain, Eric, the mystery, added up to a fellow traveler, a potential CIA agent or a potential victim, a good god or a bad god, but regardless, a someone who had his modem hooked to the other side.

Ric yelled out of the cab's open window, "Eric, where you goin'?"

Eric glanced at him, then looked down the street as if he were going to miss something. Eric turned back to him, as if he'd flipped through a Rolodex and come up with a number which was not too revealing. "The park."

"And maybe you got lost? I've never seen you outside the Rex. I thought you had a thing with your typewriter?"

"I had to get out."

"I'm off duty. Get in. I'll take you to the park."

"How's the struggle?" Eric said, getting in and slamming the door. "Who's winning?"

He made the light and shot uptown. "What struggle? Winning what?"

"Everyone's in a struggle. Inner, outer, and around the clock. In your case, it's the CIA."

Ric glanced quickly at Eric. "How do you know?"

"You tell everyone."

Eric had a point. There was the question of whether the watchers in the circle knew everyone else was watching. But that didn't matter; he had his own problem. "I suppose I do. It doesn't matter, does it? What bothers me is that they're getting ready for a big push."

"They're always getting ready for a big push. Conspiracies need climaxes."

It was deadly hot. Ric's window was rolled down and heat waves rose in all directions. Was there a big push? The only thing Eric talked about most of the time—when he did talk—was about *The Fall*, his play, which Bel told him was about Greek characters marrying their mothers and chasing each other with bazookas. Who was Eric watching a few minutes ago? "Tell me, Eric, what's this play about? I'm getting confusing rumors."

"I can't talk about it right now."

Ric passed Lincoln Center and sped up Eighth. "Why are you in the Rex?" said Ric. "It's obvious you got money."

Eric seemed to stare into an alternate universe. He shrugged, then said, "I don't know enough, Ric. I need material."

"Just what I was thinking. We're all watching each other."

"Then why worry about the CIA?"

"My story is different."

"We know. Cuba, the Bay of Pigs, the double-cross. You tell everyone. But if you're worried about the CIA in the Rex, maybe you'd be happier someplace else."

Ric thought, *Wouldn't he like that?*

Ric dropped Eric off near Seventieth, and he watched him head towards the boat ramp; then Ric drove past the Dakota and headed down the west side towards his drop-off.

That day, the bike messengers who lived in 308—Manfred, Weak, and Willie—were outside the Moat talking to Brucie and gave him those glances which Ric had gotten used to. Of course they watched him; it was perfect. But what he hadn't realized was the complexity of the surveillance. There were the Russians and Georgie. Wasn't it how terrorist cells were organized, so that no one knew exactly what was going on? Wasn't that how the Basques did it? The Red Army? The Shining Path? They were built of cells with the most fragile hooks to the next, with bonds so thin that they were easily ruptured leaving agents alone and isolated.

What began to bother him was that Eric eclipsed his worry about the CIA. It was almost as if they'd distracted him from his main course. Or were they all linked? And what, or who, was the link? He began to see it was the bike messengers. Their very name was obviously an acrostic for something like "me Kissinger," a code from a source buried deep in the hellhole of Nixon's psyche.

But there was more afoot than suspicion that night.

Bugs everywhere. There were four dead ones on the sink, four or five others slipped like brown phantoms past his roach motels, and there was one doing a weird mambo in front of his alarm clock.

\* \* \*

Ricardo Montes watched the loose group of people outside the entrance to the Main Reading Room at the New York Public Library then, senses tuned to a state of high alert, walked down the marble corridor to the men's restroom where he checked the stalls, the windows, and the back of the mirror with practiced movements.

Where was the bug? It didn't matter, did it?

He took a fortune-cookie slip out of his pocket on which was scribbled "time flies like an arrow, fruit flies like bananas," put his initials on it, and placed it underneath the toilet bowl in the first stall.

The arching marble corridor was empty when he left. In a few minutes, Ric aimed his cab north. He was cruising up Broadway when he saw him. He was skinny, sported flashy orange gym shoes, an orange reflector on his helmet, and wore a fake beard black as coal. He was riding a mountain bike—the vehicle of choice for bike messengers—patched over with orange reflecting tape.

Beardo looked like a Castro caricature. Were they mocking him?

He angled in back of Beardo at a red light. He timed the turn and just as the light changed, gunned the cab, then pumped the steering a fraction to the right. Ric heard the satisfying crunch of a bicycle wheel. His rearview mirror showed him the destruction was complete, Beardo a stick figure with his arms punching the sky.

It was a rare moment of satisfaction, a victory in a war waged every day. He'd always hated bike messengers and, in the last few days, they had become more than a traffic nemesis.

Ric hummed to himself as he cruised along the park finally shooting west down 105th and back east along 106th where he pulled in front of an Upper West Side welfare office. Frieda was waiting. Frieda was her usual self, that is going in ten directions at once, in and out of her purse, telling him to slow down, talking, rolling down the window, and trying to light an Old Gold. Once he'd thought that Frieda could be CIA, but he couldn't imagine any operative being that ditzy.

Frieda said, "To the Village, the night is on me. And drive by Times Square."

"You want a Triple XXX?"

"Don't make this complicated."

Times Square. Why did it always come back to Times Square? First there was Eric, now Frieda. He drove down Broadway, then took a right on Forty-second.

"Looking for anyone special?" said Ric.

"Someone from work. Big guy, sparse hair, horse face, wears ties with boobs on them. Somebody from work said they saw him here."

"Quite a department you work for."

"Fight with." Frieda slumped back in cushions. "Okay, I'm not going to spend my entire night with work craziness. I've exorcised my suspicions."

Ric said, "I gotta do something at the library; won't take long."

Ric turned back on Forty-first and parked on the side, near Fifth. He ran up to the second floor to check his message. It was weird but not unexpected. His message wasn't there. Instead, there was a roach, a big one, whose antennae waved at him, almost as if he were trying to tell him something. Ric stomped him. A few seconds later, his footsteps echoed down the marble corridors.

Frieda didn't look exactly uncurious when he came back.

"Good book?" she said.

He pulled away. A few seconds later, the library lions faded in the rearview mirror. His gaze settled on Frieda. She had an oval face, sloe eyes, and a ton of dark curls, a few silvered. "It wasn't a book, and it was gone."

"What was gone?"

He wondered if he should tell her everything. He didn't think it mattered. "My note."

"Tell me!" Frieda said, shaking her curls.

Ric wheeled right on Twenty-third. "An hour ago, I put a note in the men's room at the library. When I checked, it was gone." He decided not to tell her about the roach.

"And?"

It was what he wanted; but when he thought about it, he wasn't sure what it meant. "Sometimes they pick them up, sometimes they don't."

"It was a janitor."

"No."

"Who?"

Ric shook his head, exasperated. "C'mon Frieda, the CIA..."

"We're going to need tankards of Libres tonight."

35

Frieda tried to tell him it was a coincidence from the West Side cabbie barn to Frieda's dive, the Cave, which that night had its usual allotment of smoke, mournful songs, sawdust, drunks, and people sobbing in their beer.

Frieda set up the Cuba Libres, and he talked more than he'd wanted. "I work out every day," he said. He paused, swirled the rum and Coke around a cube, and took a quick sip of the cold, sugary liquid. "I do curl-ups, sit-ups...I get into a rhythm. I dream I'm in a café in Girón smoking a cigar and watching women make pigeon tracks in the sand of a white beach."

"Don't keep me hanging on every word! I'll have a heart attack."

"Then they become women and men in camouflage, then gray suits, whose smiles are like prison slits. They surround me and I pick out faces of Brucie or Ivan—"

"These women turn into Brucie and Ivan?"

"They did it."

"The women or Brucie and Ivan?"

"The Bay of Pigs. There was the pretense of friendship, information, support...but *la lucha* for a free Cuba was just a cog, a tiny cog in their game." Ric sighed and watched a crowd of people pushing in the door. He tried to distract himself. But the memory was sometimes too fresh, too painful. The memories wound through the years, through a thousand cab rides, through a thousand throwaway lines, a theme of betrayal and pursuit.

"The Bay of Pigs was thirty years ago."

"Doesn't make sense, does it? I was the one who was betrayed. Why would they follow me? It took me a long time to figure that out." He told her to come closer, and she bent over the table. "An oil exec told me in Chicago. The real secret is to keep the game going! Following me is just part of a game played by psychotics in blindfolds."

Frieda said, "I wonder if this is the big year. I'm always ready to be paranoid, but then I realize I am paranoid. Shouldn't we all be? Everyone with half a brain is plotting takeovers or how to cheat on his wife. There's a scene from *The Thirty-nine Steps* where the milkman doesn't believe the truth but soaks up an outrageous lie. We're like that; the truth is too tame for hot-shot heroes."

Ric said, "I used to watch my gold spider swing on the rearview mirror and write letters to Reagan or Bush. But they are so crazy they believe they're right, like the ones who pass lie detector tests because they know the earth is flat or women are aliens."

"Brucie and Ivan aren't smart enough to be agents. Even the CIA has standards."

"They asked me what I know that's so important. That's the test; if they think I'm crazy, they're OK. If they ask me what I know, they're CIA."

"Some test." Frieda pulled a new pack of Old Golds out of a purse the size of New Jersey and lit one. "Jews have a right to be paranoid— look what happened to us."

"Now they're right next to me."

"The bike messengers?"

"They're the perfect agents with their beepers, walkie-talkies, and bikes. Now they can track every move in my room!"

Frieda yelled, "Johnny, Cuba Libres!"

It was a long night. Ric called a driver to give them a ride back to the Rex. He was ready to call it a night, except Frieda opened a bottle of merlot and took him to the roof, her roof. Frieda was the roof, the garden, and the garden was Frieda. Everyone else was a hanger-on, there to witness the Frieda whirlwind and compliment her on her plants. Except that night some of the plants nearest the door were dug up and thrown on the runners. They looked dead with black clumps of dirt around the stems and the flowers wilted, left there like a cat leaving a rat for its master.

"Son-of-a-bitch." Frieda bent over and touched the crumbling root ball of a Gerber Daisy.

"See." He said that automatically, but when he thought of it, he wondered exactly why someone would target Frieda. Unless Frieda was right about everybody plotting.

"See what? What I see is someone's sabotaging my garden."

"Who?"

"It could be anyone...the druggies on five, some discontented soul on seven. I'm never here during the day."

"They have mikes and bugs everywhere."

"So many theys."

"These people get what they want..."

Frieda sighed. "It's like blowing in the wind. The machine grinds out the malls and Big Macs. We adopt local paranoias, so we can forget we're helpless to stop the machine. Whenever I think of the Rex, I worry about—and why should I have to worry?—about long-term people leaving and why. Luce: What about her? She was a stalwart. Gone. I suppose it was inevitable."

Frieda shook her head and plunged her hand in potting soil. Ric drank a glass of Frieda's merlot and watched Frieda re-pot the flowers and water them. When she finished she sat down and they listened to the East Side sounds and watched the penumbra of lights, which were what he imagined the aurora borealis was like, like a pulsating arch, and felt closer to Frieda because that night they were both paranoid.

When he left Frieda and approached his room, he realized that he'd forgotten the bugs. He didn't forget for long; there were twice as many as yesterday.

Sure he'd told Eric of the big push. But why had the roaches targeted his room? He interrogated a roach in a roach motel bent in supplication towards some blank-eyed cell leader.

The roach was good; he didn't talk.

Ric caught himself. Was he getting carried away? He was talking to roaches. On the surface that didn't seem too healthy. Perhaps that's what they wanted! Perhaps they wanted to drive him over the edge as part of a scheme to drive *la lucha* into the asylums! They'd done it in Russia for years.

Ric decided as he went to bed that night with the lights on and the motels in place, that he would not let—could not let!—the CIA drive him insane. *La lucha*—the fight on all fronts against the plots—continued, and he as an *exilio*, a brave *exilio*, would carry that fight to the furthest lengths of his sanity.

\* \* \*

Ric bought black disks—they reminded him of disks that ninjas used except that they didn't have razor-sharp edges—and spread them throughout his room. It was funny seeing them there, those black little disks near his sandals in the closet, under the bed, or next to the mirror. He expected that soon the roaches would be gone.

The next night, he found ten dead ones on the sink and five others slipping under the fridge. There were two more in the closet and one on the wall near the window.

Ric was puzzled. He talked to John Farmer and Bill the handyman. John said they had bugs, but they talked of two and three roaches as if the world were at an end. He had twenty in one night! The other thing that worried him was when they talked about the messengers. They were right, but the messengers were more than just slobs. They were part of the plot; but which plot? The whole business made him edgy. He started getting fidgety when he drove, thinking that there were roaches in his beads or his shirt.

He began writing down daily counts.

When his count reached forty, he stopped in the Mason Hardware in Tribeca. He roamed their aisles looking at new contraptions and bought ammunition. He bought more disks, an entire strip of brown roach motels, special pellets, spray, and finally the foolproof boric acid, which, if the chemicals and motels failed, rotted their stomachs and shriveled their legs.

Ric contemplated his supply before putting it out. There was something strange about the roaches. They started with one or two, and they increased geometrically until they began populating not just his room, but his head. He didn't have time to worry about the CIA!

He decided to take a shower before he put on his gloves and laid out his defenses. He got his towel, soap, his special shampoo, slipped out, and locked his door. The next door was open and he saw two of the bike messengers, Weak and Willie, popping their fingers and listening to headphones. He also saw a large garbage bag on the floor with food and cans spilling out and roaches crawling out of the bag and playing on it. He saw that some had started up the wall and were spreading out towards the door.

The shower on his side was occupied, so Ric took the one on the Farmers' side. As he laid out his toiletries on the toilet lid, he thought of what he'd seen. Messengers, missing messages, the CIA, roaches. The ideas spun around his head as he turned on the water. While the water sluiced off his brown back and puddled under his toes, he got the idea.

It was an elaborate plot—no, system. It was what he'd told Frieda. There was a system, and there was systematic surveillance. The watchers and the watched.

CIA messengers were breeding and sending roaches against him! The games had been serious and comic. Sometimes they used more operatives; other times they let him alone. When you let up your vigilance, the CIA came back like a malarial infection.

His theory was confirmed in the next few days as he watched the roach population in his room skyrocket from forty to close to a hundred. And he knew there were more. He remembered what Frieda had said once: if you have one, you have a thousand. He did the calculation. If Frieda were right, he had a hundred thousand roaches targeting his room.

The CIA were trying to force him to his knees using bugs he hated. Should he give in and confess he had nothing to tell? No! He was Cuban, fighter, *exilio*!

* * *

Rudi looked up and faced the Farmers, Bill the handyman, and the quiet guy in 305.

"How can I help?" It was bad when they came in threes and fours.

The older man who looked liked John Carradine, John Farmer, lowered his head and sneezed into a handkerchief. "We noticed the first bugs about a week ago."

"Exactly six days ago." Melissa looked stronger, as if she gathered the energy John had lost to his cold.

"Whatever, whatever. One day doesn't matter—can't you see that!" John had slipped into the Moat last evening and shook his head about Melissa for an hour with a very drunk Gino. "She's been particularly obnoxious lately. Every time I say something, she's on it, her nose dipping and impaling every statement like a swordfish." Gino shook his head as if he knew only too well.

"It's a war, you see, a war I have to lose because she's promised herself that she'll outlast me. Who will be right then?" Gino folded his arms and rested his chin on them. His bald head reflected the pinks and blues from the Moat's jukebox. "What if I've been right, down to the last word, and the last connective, but she lives longer—who would be right then?"

Bill, the handyman, came to John's rescue. "I told you about the bugs on the third floor."

"I talked to the messengers—there's only supposed to be one there in the first place. I told them they had to clean up and not live like pigs."

John leaned over but turned to his wife before he spoke to Rudi. "Dear."

"What is it now?" she snapped.

"Let me tell Rudi what we think is happening, and then you can tell your version."

"If we have different versions, it's like we don't know what's going on—isn't it?" Her lips pursed as if he wouldn't be Mr. Carradine for some time.

Bill: "They're crawling over the hallway like it was an interstate highway!"

Wayne: "They've targeted my fridge, like they're on a military campaign. It's like they're super-roaches! Yesterday, I found one in the takeout in my fridge!"

"It's that Cuban, Rudi," said Melissa, pursing her mouth and wagging a bony finger.

"Thank you for coming, Melissa," said John. "But we decided it was the messengers—remember? And Rudi just said he talked to them. Do you need a transcript?"

"Of course, the messengers," said Melissa. "I don't know what came over me. But I won't stand being picked on!"

"Rudi," the actor bent over, his brows almost touching the side of the half-oval. "Ric is starting to act a little strange. You know, he lives right next to the messengers. There must be some pretty big bugs in his place. He's starting to talk to himself, and we hear strange noises coming from his room. He's starting to rattle things."

"You gotta get rid of those messengers!" said Wayne.

"And that Cuban!" said Melissa.

John closed his eyes. When he opened them, he looked at Melissa, then turned to Rudi. "Ric is suffering worse than we are. I think it's driving him bananas."

"I know your floor," said Rudi. "And I hate bugs. I remember them from…Believe me, we're going to get rid of those bugs. If I have to, I'll get rid of the messengers."

Melissa said, "And the—"

"Not the Cuban!" shouted John.

Melissa's face froze into a mask and she muttered to herself, as if she were making a promise, a deadly promise.

The detachment from the third floor turned en masse and walked slowly to the elevator. Their spirits were down, but they held out the slim hope that Rudi could return their floor to its pristine state.

* * *

Ric had a mission. He'd played games—wasn't that what the US of A wanted?—too long. He'd left messages and made feeble attempts to pull it all together, but it was spiritual. His self-imposed mission of not revealing the secret that he had nothing to reveal was not enough. He needed a real enemy, something more substantial than planting messages and detecting and deflecting CIA psyche games. Fighting the messengers on the street gave him a frisson of pleasure, but it wasn't enough.

Finally he had roaches.

He began to see the roaches as not simply sent by the CIA, but as agents themselves. He didn't try to explain this last notion in great depth. He thought that perhaps to explore it too deeply might be insanity and might be exactly what they wanted! But he began seeing each new brown body as a pseudo-agent sent to drive him mad. And sanity meant the total destruction—total destruction!—of every single roach.

The first night he put out more of the little black disks, although they hadn't worked that well. He was dealing with roaches of a special sort, which were not to be killed by conventional methods, or even one method.

He didn't see any change the first night.

The second night, he scattered roach motels throughout his room, especially around the sink, the place he hated seeing them. The motels never worked entirely, but they did give him an opportunity to observe his foes. He watched for hours as they died, stuck in that sticky glue in the motel. At the end, they were husks tilted towards the glue as if they were bowing or making a weird obeisance to a primitive spirit.

He cut a roach motel in half and observed his enemies closely. They looked surprisingly like ordinary roaches. How could you train roaches? There was only one organization in the world that had the resources, will, and power to do that. The CIA—how he hated them.

The third night, he decided to rest, as if he were a god faced with an especially arduous task of creation. He turned the lights off. He had a shift at five and needed his sleep.

But Ric was restless. The battle had left him tense and excited. It was tough to sleep when you had a mission. At two he decided to get up and see what his traps had produced. He turned on the light and after rubbing his brown eyes with an equally brown fist, was greeted with an astounding sight: ten or fifteen roaches crawled over his ceiling; one crawled down towards his bed. The others sprayed out in a fan from the wall he shared with the CIA messengers.

He watched them crawling over the ceiling and realized that for the first time in his long fight with the CIA that it was all-out war.

He took down his exercise pad and after shaking two roaches out of it, put it in the middle of the floor and assumed the Lotus position he used when he wanted to think. He closed his eyes, and his head was immediately filled with a thin strip of beach and a bloody ocean. The promise, the tragedy, the continuing tragedy. He'd made a mistake; he should have stayed in Miami and fought to go back. He would have had other *exilos* to talk to. They would have joked, marched and fought the US of A, and failed together. Going against the US of A on his own was too much for any man. He remembered the gradual discovery he was being watched. There was a blur of blond hair and white teeth, posters of white teeth, smiling at him like rows of gravestones, and behind the teeth, the reality of the CIA, the probing, the empty game. He couldn't afford a defeat; he felt the force of those other *exilos* well up and surge though his body. He was Ricardo Montes, symbol, fighter, ready to wage a last battle against an entrenched pervasive enemy.

Ric opened his eyes. A large roach at the end of the mat looked back at him. It was motionless, content. Ric thought he detected a mocking smile on its face, the face of one of the bicycle messengers. His brown hand came down in a swift, sudden blow and he crushed the roach under his fist.

43

That was it—no compromise, no hostages, no prisoners. The ground rules had been laid out; his enemy had mocked him. He would annihilate him—¡*Cuba Libre!*

It was two-thirty Thursday morning and he was tired, but he couldn't wait. He got the spackling and the little brown trowel and started his campaign. He examined every crevice in the wall he shared with the agents and carefully began filling in the cracks. The sink bothered him the most—he hated finding roaches on the soap and in his toothbrush!—and he spent an hour there. When he finished, the sink looked like it was stuck on the wall with spackling.

He cut open the boric acid. The boric acid was his great secret—if they couldn't walk, they couldn't crawl, they couldn't reproduce, they couldn't bother him. The boric acid became his line of second defense. He moved his bed and measured lines of boric acid along the perimeter of his room. He poured a thin line along the spackling, thinking that an especially strong roach might eat or wiggle through, but the boric acid would get him.

Finally, for his bed, he went high tech. He'd bought state-of-the-art sonars that drove roaches away and spread them around his bed and turned them all on at once.

He left at four-thirty for his five o'clock shift, but he couldn't wait to get back and see what his handiwork had produced. How could there be any new roaches? He knew, of course, that the ones inside could reproduce, and for that he had another plan. The grand plan was to get one of those bombs that meant you had to leave your room for twelve hours.

\* \* \*

Ric talked to Rudi after his shift. Ric was tired, more tired than he'd been in a long time, but he felt on the edge of winning a battle in a war that stretched from the sandy beaches of the Bay of Pigs into a dim future. It would keep him going if he could win a battle now and then.

It was an inferno of a day. Ric didn't sweat easily, but a trickle edged past his ear and disappeared in his patterned blue shirt. "Rudi, I got a problem."

"What's the problem?"

"Roaches, billions of them. They're not coming in anymore. But I still have a lot in the room. I need one of those bombs."

Rudi was tired, as usual, but he tried to be conciliatory. "Everybody's got a lot of them."

"This is a special case, a very special case."

"I know about the messengers."

Ric cocked his head towards Rudi. "You know about the messengers?"

Rudi nodded. "I told 'em—either they move or get better habits. The whole floor complained—Bill, the Farmers, what's-his-name in 305. You're not alone."

"They don't know what I know. Those guys are not ordinary guys."

"CIA?" Rudi mopped his face with a lank handkerchief. Rudi wasn't looking forward to the fall and winter. The Rex was becoming precarious. Another developer wanted the Rex, and his partners were wavering. The Rex was a lone leaf dangling on a leafless tree.

"What else?" said Ric.

"The CIA can't be after everybody on the floor!"

"They must have lost control of the roaches. Just give me the bomb."

Rudi sighed. "Give me a few days. If it's as bad, we'll take radical steps."

"Sure."

Ric smiled as he headed for the elevator. Sure Rudi would help. Ric knew he was slightly crazy, but not that crazy. Too many things were adding up. The messages, the messengers, the bugs.

The bugs. They were on the walls, on the carpet. There were twenty on his sink; they crawled over his bed. He felt weak in his knees. His eyes teared. Ric fell to his knees and cried, big sobs that ricocheted off the wall and made the Farmers pause in their evening libation.

Then he got mad. He threw his backrest against the wall. They were close to breaking him, but they hadn't counted on one thing: he couldn't break.

That night Ric got primitive.

He took his sheets to the laundry in the basement. He piled his sheets in the washer and added a double dose of Tide and dialed the water to

"Hot." Upstairs, while the roaches in the basement were spinning and drowning, he put out more disks, more motels, more boric acid. He sprayed everywhere—in his cups, on his toothbrush, inside the fridge. Finally he took out two stiff fly swatters. He dipped them in boric acid and made them into roach killers.

*Whap...whap, whap, whap.*

He got good at getting more than one at a time.

*Whap...whap, whap.*

When the bodies littered his floor, he did disposal and started again.

*Whap...whap, whap, whap, whap.*

He spent most of the night watching for roaches and swatting—sometimes the roach wasn't dead and wiggled, crisscrossed by lines of boric acid that ate away his antennae and corroded the legs. Towards his shift at five, he'd done a lot—there weren't any roaches in sight, and he felt he'd won a small victory over the immense forces of the CIA and their insect allies. There were fewer agents on the street too. It was as if he'd destroyed so many in his room that they needed reinforcements.

He was exhausted, but happy, when he came back from his shift late Friday afternoon.

There were ten roaches in the alcove, and they looked sick. The tide had turned. He stayed up all night driving the nails into the coffin of the roach conspiracy.

*Whap...whap, whap, whap.*

Ric felt good and did that thing he saw on the street—the "high five"—with himself. He danced the samba around his room.

The next night was better. There were still a few hardy ones around the sink, and he poured boric acid into the shelves and spread it like sand under his bed. He noticed, again, there were fewer messengers on the street. He decided that the CIA had turned the messengers into roaches and the more he killed, the fewer messengers there were!

The next night, he found one roach.

*Whap, whap, whap, whap.*

The rest of the night was calm, not a single new roach. He didn't need Rudi, he didn't need anybody—he did it himself. He'd done it—he'd stopped the invasion and he'd stopped the CIA—he'd won his first victory. He was drained but happy when he grabbed his beads and headed out for the garage Monday morning. Gino snored at the desk, pudgy arms folded around his bald head. The gray light felt like rain in the small window of the front door. Ric felt that somehow he'd fought himself free. He felt at peace.

* * *

Rudi put aside the note so he would be sure to tell Ric. The neighbors had complained so bitterly about the roaches that he did a rare thing: he evicted the messengers. It was hard because he needed residents badly, but it wasn't worth an entire floor. He'd gone in himself and picked up food off the floor and the black garbage bag full of rotting food, cans, toilet paper, and cigarette butts.

He and Bill made the place spotless. They disinfected, bombed, and spackled. They wanted the third floor the way it was before the messengers came.

Rudi left a message on Ric's door and waited to tell him when he got off.

What he got was the police.

"You know a Ricardo Montes?"

"What in God's name has happened?" Rudi had that feeling about Ric. It was a bad year—maybe the worst—and anything that could happen would happen.

"Fell asleep after he dropped off a passenger at..." The cop squinted at his notebook. "...Broadway and Duane. The guy said he was funny and happy and talked about beating Bush and the CIA. The guy watched him drive away. Ran into a telephone pole."

"Where is he?"

"St. Vincent's, ICU. Was he on anything?"

"He was a very clean-cut kid. Kid? He was over 50, but he seemed to be a kid."

"Never grew up. We have to go."

Rudi watched the police walk by Brucie. Then he wiped his head with his white handkerchief and brought out the big ledger. He opened it to 310 and looked at Ricardo Montes' name through his thick glasses.

47

Rudi had developed a protective shell in his years at the Rex, but there was always a lag when something happened, a few seconds when he was more vulnerable to something like pity or sorrow. He'd known people who lived with their obsessions. It helped them put a face on the emptiness.

Rudi sighed, watched the BMWs and Jaguars speed past the Rex and seemed to recollect what he had to do. He put a question mark next to Ric's name, closed the ledger, and picked up the phone to call St. Vincent's.

# Joey

Joey Malini shook the cocaine out of the plastic bag. It spread over the mirror as if blown there by the wind. Joey inched the chair close to the table. He leaned over a mirror and diced up the coke and carefully made two parallel tracks.

Whenever he saw coke on a mirror, he always thought of snow and mountains. The coke tracks, although raised, made him think of skiing. He guessed it was an obsession; that's what the psyche people would say. Or maybe everyone thought of snow and the mountains. He didn't care what anyone else thought. For him it was the snow, mountains, skiing.

Barbie Collins said, "Let's see how good this stuff is." She leaned over the mirror, her blond hair swinging down to hide her face. She snorted two lines. She threw her head back, sniffled, and rubbed her hand across her nose. "That's the stuff."

Barbie was as tall as Joey, lithe, almost thin, but with a strong dancer's body: white perfectly curved legs, heavy breasts, and a mass of blond hair that spilled down her back that she liked to shake, like a horse. Young, everyone said she looked like the real doll. They made her keep the name in the clubs, but it was silly, especially after what she'd been through.

Joey was her opposite. He was short and thick with black hair oiled and smoothed back and a small face he tilted to one side, as if he didn't trust anything he heard for the first time.

Barbie sauntered over, pulled up a chair, and sat down at the window. She shook a cigarette out of a gold cigarette case and lighted it with a gold lighter. The smoke drifted out the window. It was late afternoon, and people walked the streets of Kip's Bay clear in the light, shades in the shadows. Cars piled up at red lights, then raced south down Lexington towards Gramercy Park. Across Lexington at the Olympia, the high-floor windows sparkled golden, and on street level a doorman inclined his head to a couple and held open the door.

Joey made two thick tracks.

He leaned down, his face inches from the mirror, his eye tilted, the reflection from the window framing the coke, the Olympia a mountain scoring the blue sky.

*Whoosh.*

He floated; he was light fracturing, dipping, sparking.

Barbie stubbed out her cigarette on the ledge, drew the shade partially down, picked up her case and lighter, got up and walked slowly to the bed. She put the case and lighter on the small night stand, kicked off her shoes, and took off her top, skirt, bra, and panties, letting them drop to the floor one by one. She eased into bed pulling the sheet over her.

The light through the shade made the room glow a faded yellow. Joey rotated his head towards the bed. Barbie lay on the bed, the sheet over her body, her legs and arms poking out like pseudo pods. "It's funny," Joey said. "I've never been skiing, but I know what it's like in the mountains, having the wind in your hair, feeling the wind cold against your face, red cap tight over your head, ski jacket open."

Barbie spoke to the ceiling. "You got some imagination."

He'd never liked being outdoors, nature, that whole thing. But he liked *imagining* the snow, the mountain, skiing. He never told Barbie everything he imagined, the trees, the mountaintops craggy but topped off with snow, the river breaking up the way it did in that TV documentary. Mostly he liked flying down the mountain. Joey chuckled to himself. He supposed he liked the *idea* of skiing, of the mountains. If he ever went skiing, he'd probably do a run, pose with the girls smiling with their white teeth, and get drunk in a warming house, or hut, and imagine what it was like outside.

"Joey, I feel horny."

Joey looked around the darkened room, the chest of drawers with the loose handle, the small TV, the single bed, Barbie's clothes clumped on the floor. The Rex was okay before Barbie. Joey laughed—Before Barbie, BB, just like BC! Yeah, it was okay before Barbie. Time to go up in the world. He'd lived in small places. One day, he'd be in the Olympia, maybe the penthouse, a big place. He'd live in style, have parties, invite lawyers and stockbrokers.

Joey made a new track but paused, thinking back. Two months ago his hands were black crabs. Ricky would tell him to change the oil, and his hands grew into black crabs with tiny white patches of skin. He remembered the oil pit, the cars streaming by, later shooting the shit in

Maud's Diner. It wasn't a bad life; it was a nowhere life. His father worked in a garage for thirty years, for nothing, for a bunch of screaming kids, a tiny house in Queens, a mortgage. To check out at fifty-five. Some life.

"Joey!"

"Right away, babe."

*Whoosh.*

Ozone. Universe.

A toilet flushed. Joey's spirit squeezed shut. He lived on the fuckin' fifth floor of the Rex! Fuckin' toilets, fuckin' bugs, fuckin' people.

Joey glanced quickly at Barbie and saw she was annoyed. He diced up a quick line.

*Whoosh.*

Wind blew his hair straight back, cold against his open jacket.

"Come here, Joey." Barbie arched her back and slowly spread her knees apart, making a sail of the sheet. She pouted at Joey and licked her finger.

Joey's head tingled. Little blue lights popped like firecrackers. The long slope, cap tight, the tracks, the mountains.

Joey kicked the chair back, took off his jeans and shorts, stepped over and leaned down towards Barbie, his cock swinging close to her breast.

Barbie kicked off the sheet, angled her left leg over his back and moved him into the bed, where she wrapped her legs around him. She brought him down so his face was inches from hers. Joey felt his cock harden and he slipped it in. Barbie felt like velvet; she always did. Barbie bucked and he worked her and worked her and worked her. It was like sliding down that slope slow and easy at first then hitting top speed, snow flying in his hot face, stinging his red cheeks, jacket open, and that fucking red cap. Then he gave it to her, exploded, his head arched high towards the ceiling.

He panted breathless for a few seconds then rolled off Barbie towards the wall.

Barbie said, "Wow. You still got it."

Joey, breathing hard, said, "Never lost it."

Barbie pulled the covers back over her breasts. She found the cigarette case with her hand, took a cigarette out of the case, and felt for the lighter. A plume rose towards a crack in the ceiling. "Joey—what do you worry about?"

Joey, naked, turned his head towards her. "That's a kinda general question. I don't worry about much. Let's see. Cops? Nah, I got that down. My supplier. Yeah, I worry about Manuel Wetback. We had a couple problems, but he seems okay now."

"What problems?"

"Couple misunderstandings. He tried to cheat me once. I weighed the batch. I told him it was short. He said I was lying, and I said I'd get another supplier. It was tense for awhile, then we patched it up. It's okay now, but if I had another supplier, I'd cut him loose."

"I guess what I meant was about the future. What do you worry about, or what do you want? Take the Rex: how long you gonna stay here?"

"Know that building out the window, the Olympia? I'm gonna live there."

Barbie frowned. "That's a big step. Place like that costs money, a lot of money."

Joey shook his head. "Well that's my plan."

Barbie looked for the ashtray on the night stand, found it, and stubbed out her cigarette. "A lot of us have big plans, and a lot of them don't work out."

"I know that. Mine will."

He met Barbie in Sally Mae's two weeks ago. He'd spent too much time and too much money in Times Square and places like Sally's. Times Square was kinda like those machines where you pump in a ton of money and sometimes get a prize and sometimes not. He finally nailed a prize: Barbie. He liked listening to her stories of fights, stupid tourists, celebrities. They both talked about moving, on moving up to another level.

Joey yawned, "What a fuckin' long day. I musta been across town ten times. I'm blasted and it's only seven."

Barbie got up from the bed and stretched. "Gotta go."

"You going home?"

"Probably. I gotta work tomorrow."

"You musta tired me out." Joey yawned and closed his eyes.

Barbie picked up her clothes and put them on. She turned on the light in the alcove and combed her hair. She saw a twinkle in one eye in the mirror and laughed silently. She liked sex, and she liked sex with Joey, but her time with him was about up. Barbie Act 2 was about to start. She didn't know what Act 2 was about, but it had to be better than Act 1.

Barbie hooked her bra, brought her mouth close to the mirror, and made short low-pitched kissing sounds at her reflection. Finally she touched the mirror with her lips, leaving a dull red kiss on the glass. She laughed silently, then a look crossed her face like a gray cloud. Barbie looked at the hillock of coke on the mirror, at Joey snoring on the bed, and picked up her frilly blouse.

Barbie buttoned her blouse but left the top button open.

She stopped and looked at Joey's back and small head. She straightened her skirt and admired her legs. She put on her coat. When she walked past the small square table she stopped, thought for a second, then opened her purse. She picked up the razor blade, opened her cigarette case, and scraped most of the coke inside.

* * *

That day a gray-haired crone stared at her as she crossed the lobby. Outside, the bald-headed creep hung out front like he was glued to a Rex pillar. The queer guy in the gray coat waited on the corner for the light. She was going east, the queer guy north up Lexington. Barbie watched him for a few seconds. Burr head, grizzled, old army coat. He looked older, seventy maybe. She supposed he'd come to some kind of accommodation with life, a life without money, without spice. She glanced back at the guy at the pillar, the old eight-story hotel. You add it all up, the Rex was a fucking asylum. She'd never live there, but Joey would. Minor dope deals and blowing all your dough in Times Square girlie joints didn't add up to diddly.

Barbie smiled grimly. And what was she doing with him?

Barbie buttoned her coat against the cold. She walked over to Third Avenue in the graying light then up to Thirty-fourth Street. It was too early for TV or food. She was high and she wanted to stay high. She pulled the top of her dun-colored coat to her throat.

Minutes later, she unbuttoned her coat and put her purse on Tommy's bar top. "Hey, Mac."

Tommy's was an old East Side bar remodeled by new money. It had a glossy black bar with black fixtures and a bar mirror that stretched to the back wall and a mirror opposite the bar that stopped where the restaurant started. A week-old spray of gladiolus and birds-of-paradise set off the end of the bar in front. Every few minutes a passerby was framed in the octagonal window.

That night, a couple sour-looking guys, one tall, one squat, nursed drinks under the flowers at the far end of the bar. Every few minutes the tall one would turn and rasp a sentence, the short one nod.

Mac was an ex-college tackle who was too small for the pros. He was built like a frog with a thick neck, bandy legs, short-cropped brown hair and small slanted eyes. He wore Vegas dealer frills and a thin black tie, which swayed when he wiped the bar.

Mac looked up from a wad of bar receipts. "Barbie."

He stepped over to her. She gave him a ritual kiss. "Isn't it about time you hired me?"

Mac frowned. "I'll think about it. What're you drinking? This one's on me."

"Vodka martini. Can you use Absolut?"

"You bet." Mac picked Absolut and vermouth off the back bar. "How's Sally Mae's?"

Barbie watched him make her drink. "I'd blow the place up if I had another job. Sweaty drunk tourists, bad breath, watered drinks. They go back to Iowa and talk about the great time they had, the girls."

Mac poured the drink, popped in an olive, and set it in front of her. He shook his head sadly. "Must be tough having your old man—"

"You get over it."

"You got a boyfriend?"

"I see a guy, but he's more like a brother. He lives in an asylum a couple blocks away."

Mac laughed and looked at Barbie, wondering if it was a joke. "Asylum?"

"They call it the Rex. It sounds more like a kennel than a hotel."

"The owner told me that ten years ago we did a big business with the Rex. It was a different place then. Now only a couple old guys who live there drop in."

"You let them in?"

"They're OK, but they don't tip so good."

"Think you'll be there one day like these guys, sitting at some bar crying in your gin and tonic about the olden golden days?"

"This is the loneliest time of the week—Sunday night in a bar on the East Side. These guys could bum anybody out. They keep asking me if I knew Dolan or Freddy or the Dizzy the shoe-shine boy. They should close this place on Sunday."

Barbie laughed. "Tell me when you have a break. I got a present."

"A present for me?"

"What's white, comes in little mounds, and loves noses?"

"Nose-fu. That's nice, but I got my own—enough to go skiing."

"Christ, another skier. You'd think it was the Winter Olympics."

The smoke enveloped them and spread towards the front of the bar. Mac hunched over his elbows on the bar top. "You work tomorrow?"

"Don't remind me. What did you have in mind?"

"How about a diversion?"

Barbie laughed. "Diversions. Yeah I know about those."

"If you stay around, I'll feed you another drink, and when I close we'll find something to eat and watch a movie at my place. I got Mel Brooks—*Young Frankenstein*."

"Baron Frankesteeeen! You sure you don't you need somebody on the weekend?" Barbie matched Mac's half-lidded eyes over her drink.

"We'd sure have a lot of customers with you around."

\* \* \*

Joey woke at nine the next morning. He had a headache from the booze, the coke, but he had to get it together. He had two deals that morning. With that dough, he'd get a larger batch from the Weasel. He stared at the table. Most of the coke was gone, the mirror empty. Where'd the coke go?

Joey frowned. He needed that coke for the deals that morning. And he had a ton of deals the next two days.

Joey got dressed and hurried to the elevator and punched "1." The elevator stopped a foot below the first floor. Joey got the folding gate open, but the door to the lobby stuck.

"Fucking elevator." He let the folding gate shut and punched the button to the basement. The elevator started and seconds later stopped with a shudder.

Joey got out. "Fuckin' relic."

A door cracked down the long corridor. Ben looked out.

Joey said, "What are you lookin' at?"

Ben shook his head, croaked a laugh, and shut the door.

"Fucking hermit." Joey hated the basement. He climbed up the stairs. After closing the door, he turned into the phone room. The single bulb cast a dim yellow radiance over phone books with pages torn out, a single chair, and cigarette butts scattered over the floor.

He closed the door, dropped in his change, and dialed the number. The numbers scratched around the phone looked like invaders closing in on a black castle.

Barbie picked up.

Joey said, "How much did we do last night? I was sure there was a truckload left."

"I didn't count, babe—you had a good time and was wasted by seven."

"I guess I was. Shit, I got to get it together today. I'll call you tomorrow."

Joey hung up. He'd counted on the rest of that batch to get ahead. With all the deals in the last month, he was close to even. Barbie was right. If he was going to live in the Olympia, he was going to need bigger deals. Maybe that day was the day; maybe that day would put him ahead for good. He had to use all of his savings, but you had to pay to play. First there was the bank, then the Weasel, then delaying his morning deals. Joey, fighting his headache, but energized, put all his change on top of the pay phone and started feeding it.

Manuel was pissed but he agreed to come over at ten with a bigger batch. Then Joey called and left messages for his clients. He hurried out of the Rex, and at ten, he was waiting in the queue at the B of A. He took out most of his money for the big batch. At ten-thirty, he saw

Manuel. By eleven, he'd cut the coke he needed for that morning and done up the baggies.

Then he got busy.

He did a deal with the blond fag on six. That's right, Eric Somebody. He hated fags, but the kid wasn't bad, just fucked up. It was in the genes anyway. You either had it, or you didn't. Then he walked to the Olympia. The doorman pissed him off; he wasn't going to let him in before he called the guy on 20. The guy at the Olympia had a classy joint, thick Persian carpets, masks, monster TV, space ship stereo. He had an awesome view of the East River.

Joey didn't like leaving the Olympia. He felt he belonged there already. Back at the Rex, he called George, a lawyer and one of his steady customers, trying to drum up business. George wanted some but had to meet him outside near his office in Madison Square Park. He hated dealing outside but hiked over to Madison Square Park anyway. Everyone in the park looked like a cop, and he was nervous, walking like his legs were made of wood. George wore a gray suit, lined rain coat, and carried a soft leather attaché case. Joey joined him, and they kicked their way through the leaves towards the playground off Twenty-third. They sat on a bench facing the Metropolitan Building. Four or five dogs chased each other. A couple kids strolled through wearing werewolf masks.

Halloween. Kid stuff.

They did the exchange: bucks for snow.

He got up, waved at the guy like he was a friend, and hurried towards Park Avenue. He felt like a speck against the Metropolitan building. He zigzagged through the avenues and streets as if there were someone following him.

He did a deal at the Giltmore and another on the West Side.

He stopped in Times Square for a couple brews. He avoided Sally Mae's because Barbie didn't like him there when she worked. That was funny, because he met her there. He understood it though; the management didn't like boyfriends hanging around.

He went to the Silver Ring instead. Times Square had electricity, crowds, bums, old movie houses, girly shows and people on the make. It was the biggest neon circus in town. When he moved to Manhattan, he hung out there all the time in places like Sally Mae's. Since he met Barbie, he didn't hang out there so much. He'd started seeing how tacky it was;

it was almost as if, if he kept going there, he'd become tacky himself.

He had one beer in the Silver Ring and watched the go-go dancers for a few minutes, then he walked back to the Rex. He was high and slightly tipsy and picked up some moo goo gai pan at a Chinese restaurant. He had started up the Rex steps when he heard sounds from the Moat and decided to stop in. He had a couple longnecks and shot the shit with Gino the fat alkie. Gino was already plastered, but he was funny, always talking about Kip's Bay being invaded by the yuppies. The Moat was okay; it felt right just like Bill's in Queens. He guessed when he lived in the Olympia, Times Square was out and so were dives like the Moat.

\* \* \*

Barbie waved a bottle of Cabernet at him. You OK, Joey?"

Joey shrugged. "Sure, sure."

Barbie frowned. "You don't look so hot."

"First, I'm wasted. Second, I can't believe we did so much coke Sunday. I thought there was a ton left."

"You always get loaded. I quit counting your tracks."

"Yeah, I suppose I do. I took out my savings to get a big batch, then worked like a clown to make my deals." Joey finished a beer, watched his biceps flex as he crushed the can, and threw it in the wastebasket. "I unloaded most of the batch I got, and I got a bag left. Say, this beer goes right through me. I'll be right back."

When Joey came back, he got out the mirror and his personal stash.

Barbie said, "Let's have a line and get it on, you little stud."

Joey made four lines.

Barbie did hers.

Joey skied.

*Whoosh.*

He floated, sailed.

Barbie frowned. "Hey pour us a glass. It's open."

Joey found two clean glasses in the alcove, poured out two glasses, and gave one to Barbie. He stood over the table and sipped the wine.

"Hey, that's good."

"What's life if you can't live a little?"

"Exactly. One of these days, we're going skiing, and we're going to live in the Olympia."

"We? Aren't we getting a little ahead of ourselves?"

"Why not?"

"There's a lot more to life than getting stoned and getting along in bed."

"Maybe we should go on a vacation. Maybe—"

"Slow down. We've only known each other for a couple weeks."

Joey, blitzed, fantasized about skiing and life in the Olympia. It was right there. They'd have parties; they'd watch the East River together. They'd have one of those racks on the Beemer and drive to the Catskills and ski. Joey imagined what it would be like standing with Barbie, skis between them, big shit-eating smiles on their faces.

"Don't worry, Joey. Right now, let's enjoy ourselves."

* * *

Tommy's restaurant had just closed. Aerobic couples and businessmen paid their bills, and two women in frilly blouses and buttoned blue suits stopped to talk near the spray of flowers at the end of the bar. A few minutes later, they strode out the door.

Barbie sat near the waitress station and crossed her legs. Mac wiped glasses that looked small in his hands. He hovered near Barbie, but left now and then to refill a drink.

Mac walked past the obsidian piano set like a totem in the back of the restaurant and disappeared through a door that said "Staff Only." Barbie took a long pull on her martini, then fished in her purse. She unzipped a hidden pocket and found the large zip-locked bag. She guessed it was about two ounces, maybe two thousand bucks worth. Nice. She knew where she could get rid of it. She dropped the bag in her purse and clicked it shut.

She almost felt sorry for Joey. He was a regular at Sally Mae's. He dropped money every night. He showed up right at a Barbie intersection, a limbo. She took him to bed, and they'd had a few laughs. She should have expected he was like everyone else, out for himself, with a basketful of boring stories and dreams. In the last few days, he'd started to seriously bore her. That's when she started seeing him as a way out, a way to that next act, a way to ditch Sally's, find a better apartment, get a new life. It came to her when Joey was in the can. He was already half-loaded and was getting careless. He'd put the bag on top of the fridge. She'd looked at it for a long second before she picked it up.

Two Macs came back. The mirror Mac snapped off when he got to the bar. Mac dusted off the bottles and put them in the back bar.

Barbie finished her drink, opened her cigarette case, took a cigarette out, and tapped it on the bar. Mac came over and lighted Barbie's cigarette.

"You got a new flick tonight?"

Mac looked sly. "I'll always have something for Barbie, especially when she brings me presents. It's that horror flick—*Fatal Attraction*."

"Sounds like fun."

* * *

Joey woke up at ten that night. Barbie was gone and he had another headache. The place looked trashed. They'd done a bunch of coke and there was still some on the mirror.

He remembered the deals he'd made that day and the day before. He had at least two ounces left. Maybe this was the time he got ahead.

Where is that last bag? He didn't remember putting it away.

Joey got up, shook his head, and walked into the closet. He checked his pack, then he walked into the alcove and opened the fridge. He moved the beer out of the way; he always put it behind the beer. Nothing but the bright fridge light. Joey frowned and looked in the cabinet above the sink. Then he searched his room from the closet to the annex, from the bedsprings to the dresser. He crawled on the floor and checked under the bed. It was gone. His last bag, the big one. The one that was going to put him ahead.

He thought back. The last deal was at the Olympia. He had it then.

The guy wanted to see it, to see if he wanted that much. Then he put it in his pack. He remembered because he zipped it in. Back, he took it out of the pack. That's when Barbie came in. He'd left it on top of the fridge and gone to the bathroom. He must have put it in the fridge.

Joey opened the fridge again and regarded the empty space. He closed the door. He sat on the bed and smoothed his short hair back as if that helped him think. He thought back. The coke that was missing Sunday night, the missing bag.

*He* didn't do that many lines, and he didn't misplace the bag.

He wasn't *that* stupid. What happened stared him in the face. His missing bag was in Barbie's purse.

Barbie had talked about going to places on Thirty-fourth. Joey threw on his jacket and checked his money. He hurried downstairs, out the door, and up Lexington. He stopped at Max's and scanned the crowd. He left and went to Walt's. Still no go. His quest was hopeless. What would he do if he found Barbie anyway? He couldn't make a scene.

He'd started back to the Rex when he saw Tommy's sign across Thirty-fourth. Joey strolled over, hesitated about going in and instead stood on his toes and looked in Tommy's octagonal window. It was breaking up, the restaurant closing. A couple at the door, a few guys nursing drinks at the bar. He'd turned to go when he saw Barbie striding towards the bar with a short guy who went in back of the bar. She looked stoned, with a weird lop-sided grin.

Joey felt his jaw harden, his heart race. He felt like rushing into Tommy's and crushing Barbie's face with his fist over and over and over.

A couple opened the door, saw him waiting, and held the door open. He shook his head no, turned and walked away.

*  *  *

Joey held his breath and called Barbie.

"You see Joey, I like you but you're getting too territorial. I need time to sort things out."

"C'mon babe. I miss you."

"I do too, Joey. I just need a little time."

Joey sighed. "Yeah sure, you're right. Anyway, that's too bad. I started thinking about what you said about getting ahead. I just got a monster batch from the Weasel on credit. This will be my biggest score. I'm going to be a lot closer to the Olympia."

"Yeah?"

"I got half a pound. We couldda gotten loaded, and I would be way ahead."

"Wow. That sounds great."

"I wouldn't have said we needed time apart, but maybe you're right. We both need a little space. I guess—"

"Wait a minute...let me rethink this. I could have been hasty. Tell you what. I'll come over this time and we'll see. We'll take it from there."

"Whatever you want, Barbie."

\* \* \*

Joey opened the door. Barbie wore a tight red dress, red shoes. The cork of a bottle of wine stuck out of a brown paper bag.

Joey said, "You always look great."

"You don't look so bad yourself. What's on the agenda? Where's this new batch?" Barbie put her purse on the night stand and took her coat off.

Joey locked the door. He took a sip of beer and watched her.

"Say, what are you looking at? Let's do some tracks, get happy."

"I'm trying to see what a thief looks like."

Barbie backed up, the back of her legs hitting the bed. "What?"

"Let's see, there's the coke you took on Sunday and the bag Tuesday."

Barbie grabbed at her bag and turned towards the door. Joey grabbed the top of her blouse, jerked her around with his left hand, wrenched her back.

Barbie, stunned, ducked her head. She mumbled, "Let me go."

Joey got ready to backhand her but stopped. He drew her close so her face was inches from his. "You know I had the worst dreams of my life last night. I thought of all the ways I could fuck you up. I remember this movie *The Grifters* and using oranges in a bag to beat somebody because it doesn't leave any marks. I thought of throwing acid in your face and breaking your arms. I thought of shooting your legs off one by one. Guess which one came in first."

Barbie's eye widened.

Joey said, "Nothing. Not a thing. It's not worth it. You're not worth it. And guess what, there's no big batch. I didn't call the Weasel. I wanted to see if you'd take the bait. I suppose you came here to rip me off again."

Joey shook his head and let go of her blouse.

Barbie looked at her purse and said, "I needed it for a new start."

Joey said, "We all need new starts."

"I took the coke on Sunday for a lark. Tuesday, don't know what came over me. It was sitting there."

"Because you'd already decided to ditch me. I learn slow, but at least I learn."

Joey went to the door. He unlocked it. He felt like asking Barbie to stay, but he knew he couldn't. He knew he had to let her go, and when he did, he'd be lonely again. He'd go back to the bars, spend his money, and think about the big score.

He said, "Maybe you will have a next act." Joey opened the door. "But I don't think so."

Barbie put on her coat and buttoned it. She grabbed her purse and coat and hurried out the door. She turned outside the door and said, "I'm sorry, Joey. You're probably right. I don't have a next act."

Joey shut the door and watched it for a few seconds. He wasn't sure what he was going to do, but he didn't want to stay in that room. He got his jacket, money, and keys. In the elevator, he paused, shrugged mentally, and punched eight instead of one.

On eight, he climbed up the stairs to the roof.

It was a cold, clear fall day. From where he was on the roof, he could see the Olympia rising into the clouds. People in the penthouse, a party.

The guys at Ricky's Garage had already put down their wrenches and screwdrivers. They'd washed the oil off their hands and had walked to Maud's Diner. Right now, they were jiving with each other and talking about their girls—it was the best part of working at the garage, shooting the shit with the guys. He talked about how he was going to make it out of there, how he had to get out of there. I'm not going to have black crabs for hands. I'm not going to die at fifty-five.

63

He walked over to the edge and looked down. On his right, skids of plants and flowers spread out south. They were withering, dying. One part of the ledge around the roof was lower, topped with the tile you see on Spanish houses. It had a little angle pointed down and looked dirty and slippery. He looked over the edge and saw all the junk people threw out their windows at the bottom in the dead space. You opened a window and threw your stuff down there; he'd done it himself.

The brick was worn—he'd never seen it before—old and worn. Drawn shades in the low building across the dead space, somebody sleeping. Joey looked up at the Olympia. At that moment, he knew he'd never live there. Maybe some day he would go skiing, but he'd never live in the Olympia.

He felt at that moment he would be happier in Queens. He'd been on edge every minute in the city, every deal…and everybody was on the make. The Weasels, the Barbies, the lawyers, the stockbrokers, the rich ones in the Olympia, the glittering ones, the enticing ones.

Ricky, the owner of Ricky's Garage, offered to make him manager before he left.

He wondered if the offer was still open.

# Rose

Rudi, Jewish, atheist, a myopic dwarf, stuffed his thick black-rimmed glasses in his salt-and-pepper hair and geared up for a holiday season. He detested the season, but bowing to what he thought was the general mood, replaced the philodendron in the spare lobby with a plastic green-blue spruce, which he festooned with miniature Christmas wreaths, tiny artificial snowballs, and asynchronously blinking red and green lights.

Some of the residents liked the tree; most did not. The inhabitants of the Rex lived on a desert island in an ocean of gentrification and were ambivalent about the season. For some, it felt like an intrusion from the greater world of Kip's Bay, from the Giltmore, the Olympia, the Kip's Bay Palace and a score of renovated buildings and high-rises stuffed with cheerful spendthrifts on buying sprees at Macy's, Tiffany, Baccarat, Bergdorf-Goodman, and Bloomingdale's.

Dr. Harry Hanson was in a depression, a lingering, battering depression, and it was more, much more, than the tree in the corner. Harry had put his thick forefinger in the wind to do a weather check on his life and found it had frozen and that the rest of his body was succumbing to frostbite. In the past few weeks, his arrest and affair with Luce a distant memory and his money dwindling, he hit bottom as Rex desk clerk. An endless number of faces paraded by the tree, out in the morning, back in the evening, like the tides. Ben, the troll from the basement, burr head stuffed deep in a tattered army jacket, roamed in and out all day looking for the ghost of Celine. The Quincys, Goofy and Olive Oyl, talked Second Coming. Gino, alcoholic, stumbled into the Moat, one of the last old bars in Kip's Bay, and lurched back.

Harry balanced his large curly head on his large soft hand and daydreamed. His liaison with Luce, however brief, had given him hope. When she left following his arrest, another Manhattan casualty, hope evaporated. If he could hold out until spring, if he could find new jobs to apply for, if, if, if...

"Harry!"

Harry's head jerked up. Rose Tutwiler, retired Garment District clerk, emerged from his right. The door slammed behind her. She hid the tree. Light haloed her antique black hat. Rose was a diminutive woman with a thin mouth, clear gray eyes, and white hair, a few strands of which escaped from under her black hat. She perched a worn purse in front of her neck, as if she were protecting the silver cross which peeked out from behind it. She had the air of a maiden aunt of dark fussy secrets.

"Time to pay the rent?" Harry drew the ledger across the worn tile counter.

"Not yet," Rose said with a firm voice. "I know it's due, but I'd like to wait till tomorrow."

Harry shrugged. "I'm sure it will be all right with Rudi; after all, you've lived here—"

"That's right, for seventeen years. But who cares about that?"

Rose smiled at Harry, looked at the Christmas tree with an edge of disgust, but then got herself in hand. The lines around her mouth tightened, and her brows dipped towards her purse.

"Anything else?" Harry replaced the ledger on the shelf behind the window. The letter boxes loomed behind Harry. The small heater in the corner made his right side hot. Out the window a few snowflakes drifted through the early evening. The streetlight on the corner rose like a beanstalk and cast wedges of light over the street and lay pale on the windowsill. People balanced packages and walked briskly in and out of soft gray shadows.

Rose glanced at the tree. "I detest this season. This tree is so hideous."

"Christmas?"

"All those people pretending to have a good time. It's an excuse to spend money, that's what it is." Rose tightened her grip on her purse as if a salesman at one of the big stores had just asked her to open it and give him all her money. "It is the time to celebrate the birth of Christ."

"If you're a Christian," said Harry. He tilted back and the desk chair creaked.

"That's right; let's be as politically correct as possible."

Harry frowned and edged back towards Rose.

Rose took a step closer to the half-oval and said apologetically, "I didn't mind it as much a few years ago when I had friends in the neighborhood—when it was a neighborhood. We'd go out on Christmas—you know they have Christmas specials in the restaurants. But all my friends have died or left. Do you know what it's like to be the last one—like a dinosaur?"

Harry had been feeling like a dinosaur himself—the frozen finger, the tide washing faces before his eye, the disappearing prospects. Christmas in New York. "Miserable time of year."

"I've been thinking for some time..."

Harry sensed Rose was about to broach her favorite subject. "About?"

Rose looked at him closely, as if she'd guessed he was humoring her. Then she rested her purse on the ledge without releasing it. "I've developed an interest in leaving—not my own leaving certainly, because that would be against the Church and wrong. At least I think it would be. But I do have a certain interest. I know you're a doctor, or used to be, and I was wondering if you could give me some advice."

Used to be. He wasn't debating that. Rose looked at him expectantly, as if he were going to supply the key ingredient in a soufflé.

Leaving? "I usually don't talk to people about 'leaving.' You do mean dying."

"Yes, yes. We call it self-deliverance, too, but I prefer 'leaving.'"

We? "'Leaving' it is. What about it?"

"What in your opinion is the best method? The safest, painless, foolproof—you know, the things one should think of."

"Well—"

"I have a book—several books—you see, and I've studied it. I think the best way is barbiturates. I've dismissed everything else. Guns and knives are too primitive, and I have a horror of hurting myself. Hanging is abhorrent—they do that to criminals. Subways are too messy, and jumping out the window is too. Those ways are violent and suited to men. They don't suit my personality, you know what I mean?"

"Well—"

"You see, I plan—hypothetically, if I were to plan. I would plan to have my favorite meal in my favorite Greek diner, Plato's. My favorites are Greek salad, spinach pie, and apple pie à la mode. Then I'd come home and get myself ready for bed, mix the barbiturates in some cold water, take them, drink some Canadian Club seltzer for better absorption, and have a final glass of Christian Brothers tawny port—looking out my window. Then—while I'm still able—I'd light a candle and arrange

67

myself in bed. I can't think of a more serene leaving, can you?"

Harry was surprised at her precision, especially about the accessories. "First of all, 'self-deliverance' is for terminally ill or incapacitated people. You look pretty fit to me." Rose was one of those thin, spry women who effortlessly lived to be ninety.

"Yes, yes—can't you go on?"

"Physicians aren't supposed to help healthy people leave—that's what I was trying to say."

"You can skip all that. I've heard the psychobabble."

"I've taken the Hippocratic oath; I don't help people leave."

Rose shook her head dismissively. "It's all theoretical, Harry. Pretend it's about someone else." The purse disgorged a small notebook and pencil. Rose opened the notebook, flipped it to a section entitled "LEAVING" in big block letters, leafed through ten pages of notes, turned over a new page, and waited.

Harry shrugged. "One of the mistakes in taking barbiturates is food. It reduces the effectiveness of the barbiturates, and if you eat too much, it could make you vomit."

"I remember that from the books." Rose pursed her mouth and flipped a page. "I'd have to wait. Anything else?"

"If I were to do it, I'd take more alcohol."

Rose flipped another page. "That's right. It can intensify the action of the barbiturates. I've thought of that. I wouldn't want to get drunk though!"

"An extra glass wouldn't hurt."

"What about dosage? That's very important. If I were to do something like that, I would want it to work. I wouldn't want to have to do it all over again."

Harry was through playing her game. He knew she wasn't serious. Rose had been beating the suicide drum for years.

Rose clamped her notebook shut and put it back into her purse. Then she waved at him, as if she were dismissing that question. "I know already. Forty Seconal should do the trick. I just wanted confirmation. Did I tell you what I'd do after the port? I'd arrange myself on the bed and go to sleep just like an angel, just like Abbey Hoffman."

"Abbey Hoffman?" Harry shook his head.

Rose turned towards the elevator but stopped and turned back to Harry.

"You know that none of that is important," said Rose seriously.

"What?"

"What we've been talking about. It's just talk, isn't it? If someone really wanted to do it—to leave—they'd find a way."

"It's an odd avocation," said Harry.

"It's just that," said Rose. "An avocation. That's what everyone thinks, isn't it?"

"I don't know what other people think."

Rose stared behind Harry, as if she were finding her words in the mailboxes. "Beyond the determination to do it, I have a real problem."

"What is that?"

Rose shook her head, vexed. "I need a helper."

"Helper?"

"It would be nice to have someone there. The problem is that you can't advertise for a helper. You have to be subtle about it; I'm so indirect nobody knows what I'm talking about."

Rose seemed too sincere, almost as if she'd thought everything out in advance. But what was the point? Harry said, "People want to know why. I want to know why. You talk as if staying isn't an option, as if it's a done deal. What's wrong with staying? You can turn your life around. You can do anything you want, within reason."

"I know, get a drug, find a group, find a therapist, do something, anything. Well I don't want to stay, I want to leave—at least, I think I want to leave—and I need a helper. There are a few people I haven't tried, mostly because I can't stand them. Imagine being helped by someone who wants you to leave!"

The phone cut Rose off, but when Harry answered it, it was dead. When he looked up, Rose had vanished.

* * *

After talking to Harry, Rose took the elevator to the sixth floor. Gino was already drunk. He'd left his door open and she could see the

Monet print on the wall, his rack of fantasy novels, scattered *Playboys*, the overflowing ashtray. She was sure that some day he would incinerate the entire building.

The Quincys, the couple in 612, were unlocking their door and said hello to her. She was civil, but the Quincys—with their bibles and Oprah—had started making fun of her. They didn't say anything outright, but she could tell that they talked of Rose Tutwiler and her "leaving" obsession behind her back. She'd talked about it for years. It certainly didn't seem as if she were going to do anything.

She used the bathroom, then settled into her room. It was the same cubbyhole she'd left two hours ago. Bed on the right, bookshelves under the room buzzer, a chest of drawers in the right corner, an alcove with a marble sink and small refrigerator in the left corner. The only bright spot was her woven Mexican rug with ropey tassels.

She poured herself a Christian Brothers tawny port and sat at the table next to the window.

Red and green lights blinked on and off in Kip's Bay row houses and high-rises. The penthouse of the Olympia was bathed in soft greens. Rose watched stick figures walk, circle, and toast each other. There was a fat man, a thin woman who kissed him and laughed, two small boys. They'd built the Olympia a year ago and since then, the neighborhood had changed more than she could have guessed. It cut off her view to the east, but more, she was constantly reminded of the change when she looked at the spire-like building with the bright lights, gleaming silver kitchens, and luxurious accommodations. She'd glanced at the new couple across Lexington with their cadmium yellow-painted kitchen and the pots and pans hanging in the air as if by magic, but they looked cross at her and closed their shades as if she were a troublesome dog who had to be shooed away.

Across from the Olympia, the Giltmore blocked her view uptown. Gazing north and east used to be one of her favorite activities, but lately all she saw were strangers and stranger buildings. It increased that loneliness that touched everything she did. The season's red and green lights mocked her with their fake friendliness.

If there was ever a time to leave...

She'd always had a morose side. Not always—since, she supposed, her father left. But in the last few years, her friends—the ones she could count on at Thanksgiving and Christmas—were gone, her photo gallery around the room buzzer a morgue. She used to take the photos down when someone died, but lately she didn't have the energy. Mabel Ratchett, sixth floor, extra-large front apartment, died six months ago of a heart attack. But Mabel still watched her, her yellowed photo curled over the top of buzzer, a thin smile on her oval face, a pink bow binding her white curls.

Lately, thoughts of her childhood on Long Island had mingled with the sharp, sunny townhouses of Kip's Bay. She'd led a postcard life until she was sixteen. Her father, George, was the most successful Aetna salesman on the east coast; her mother was good-looking, the Tutwilers the center of the neighborhood. She remembered vividly, often obsessively, the day her father waved at them, then shut the garage doors, turned on the car, and gassed himself with that new red hose. Her mother knew why he'd done it but never told her. The official reason was "financial setbacks," but Rose knew that wasn't true. She'd spun out her own reasons, of course, but it remained a mystery, the mystery of her life.

She'd always wondered what he was thinking, how he disguised what must have been a secret sorrow. How, she wondered, can somebody act so completely normal, talk to the neighbors, kiss the girls, wave at the family, and then, as if it were just another afternoon activity, shut the garage and leave forever?

At least she wouldn't have to worry about depressing the people around her—they were all gone, except her sister, Teresa. Teresa always talked about her visiting, but it was always vague, as if Teresa had to find exactly the right slot for her between the kids getting married, or re-married, babies, and vacations to exotic locations she'd never heard of. Why not call it what it was? There was too much life at Teresa's, and Teresa couldn't find time for the opposite—the grim, spare, anti-life force Rose Tutwiler carried with her like an old handbag.

Her friends chided her about her morbid streak and tried to get her to brighten up her room. Milly—before she died—tried to get her to buy a new chest of drawers. What an unnecessary expense, when she looked into it! She'd looked at posters with Georgianne—she'd pulled her photo down a year ago—to brighten up the wall, but they were all depressingly cheery, reminders of people with money having a good time. What an insult to have to look at happy people enjoying themselves!

But Mabel Ratchett forced her to admit she could have done something with her room. It hadn't changed much since she'd moved in. The walls were yellower, the floor around the leak in the radiator more warped, the stain in the sink larger.

Rudi told her he'd help her put in a nicer bed—if she bought it, naturally. Rudi was all right, but he thought she was made of money!

Time to leave, time to leave.

Leaving, like her father. He simply left—perfect, tasteful; perhaps not to those he left, but for himself. He waved good-bye as they drove away in the station wagon, smiling, just another happy day at the Tutwilers. She wondered if he'd hummed to himself as he got the new hose ready and made sure there was enough gas in the Chrysler. His strong bronzed hand rested on the steering wheel, his key chain—the one with the nude that her mother hated—hung from the ignition, a last-minute hesitation about whether he'd left anything on in the house. Whenever she thought of her father, she thought of the details—of his hands, or new shirt, or his key chain. But after going over that scene obsessively for hours, she had to stop.

She usually stopped picking over the shards of the past with the Chrysler and her father. The rest—her mother pining away and dying, the aunt she hated, a demeaning clerical job in the Garment District, the layoff, the ridiculous welfare check—was the working out of a bad dream, boring, something to be ticked off on one's fingers and forgotten.

She had the motive, the research—she'd bought books from the Hemlock Society, joined the local organization, Concern for Dying—and poured over the details. She ran over the different possibilities as if she had found an exciting new catalogue, one that presented the important—not material—things of life. Then, indulging her whim, she set about getting the means. Gradually, after complaining of sleeplessness—which was true!—she had crawled up the drug ladder from Dalmane through Equanil to arrive at the drug she wanted—Seconal. Every night she took the unopened brown bottles down. They seemed innocuous, not deadly.

She wasn't sure why, but soon she started telling people about her project—suggesting, hinting, dropping innuendos. They listened at first, tried to cheer her up, suggested therapists. But after a few months, they quit believing her.

That's when she realized she wasn't ready. She needed embroidery. The embroidery—the setting—soon became an important part of her plan: her last solitary meal at Plato's, the return to her room, her final preparations, the lethal dose of Seconal, the tawny port, Rose Tutwiler arranged with dignity on her narrow bed. The embroidery was complete, everything perfect: the intention, the dose, the embroidery, the A-to-Z planning, the serenity.

What was missing? Was there some one thing that would help her complete her project? It finally came to her: she needed a helper. But would a helper really help? She canvassed her options. Alex? Alex saw through people, and she was ruthlessness. But she didn't like her, and she suspected Alex would ridicule her. There was that strange young man with his Nietzsche philosophy. He said he was a student. She talked to him in vague terms, and he said he understood what she was saying—in theory. But she didn't know—how could she ever know another person understood what "helping" meant?

There was Ben, the troll in the basement. Of course he understood, except she couldn't stand the man. That would be worse, going out with someone you disliked. Ben wouldn't do it anyway.

Once, she thought that she should write a testament about her phantom helper, but then she didn't. She wasn't sure she'd have a helper—that would make her seem silly if someone discovered a testament about a helper who never helped and never intended to help. The whole business had become an additional burden; she wanted to leave and couldn't, and that left her to roam the halls of the Rex or sit in the lobby looking in the faces of the tenants for a helper, like that philosopher and his lamp looking for an honest man.

\* \* \*

Rose walked by the Lord and Taylor windows. It was night, the snow drifted, and she watched old and young faces strain to catch a glimpse of Santas with ruddy cheeks and squads of elves with pointed feet and hats. There were bright red and green mountains of toys and sleighs in dreamscapes of glittering plastic snow and mounds of goodies under gingerbread trees. It was a modern-day Dickens Christmas thought Rose, smug and paternalistic. It was a rich confection baked every year by gleeful advertisers. How much of it was real? But that day, Rose felt her cynicism ebb. Why should she object to what other people did? She may be morbid and morose, but was she a misanthrope?

She hadn't thought of going to Plato's, but she found herself there facing a busy Greek diner humming with the sounds of people enjoying themselves. She moved three times—her favorite booth in the back was taken; the second faced a window and the reflection of a tiny, lonely woman. The third had a loose spring, but the fourth was all right, except the waiters seemed to have an amusing time at her expense.

She crooked her finger at Philo. Philo frowned and made his way through the other diners to her table. "I don't want one of your Christmas specials, Philo! Ham with all the trimmings—that's for them!"

"Of course, Rose."

"Don't placate me! It's a special day for me—can you understand that? I want a fresh spinach pie, not one made last week!"

"You got it," Philo said, winking at her.

She knew he *was* placating her, but she didn't mind that night. She tucked her purse next to her and dismissed him with a wave of her hand. "We'll see."

Philo seemed to get the message, and she settled in, shaking her head at the waiters who smiled around her like predatory birds. The Greek salad was good and, she was happy to find, so was the spinach pie. The apple pie à la mode was good too. It made her feel as if she'd rescued the day from her abortive conversation with Harry. Why did she continue to beat that dead horse? She announced it was a sham to herself, then forgot.

She walked the two long city blocks back to the Rex. It wasn't snowing that night, except the wind was making snowflakes glitter in the cones of light on Lexington. Gino had replaced Harry at the desk, and she almost decided to stop. But then she knew Gino was probably loaded. She had complained to Rudi about him.

Gino frowned at her as she passed the square clerk's window.

The elevator jerked up the floors. It stopped on four, but no one was there, and it wouldn't start when she punched six. She walked up the last two floors.

Rose stored her hat in the closet and hid her purse in the corner. She sat at the window. She didn't feel alone, more estranged. At eighty-thirty she got ready for bed. She pulled the covers up and was about to switch off the light, but she held her hand. A thought came to her. Ben was the one person who knew what she was trying to do.

She had to see him, whether he wanted to help her or not. She got dressed and walked down six flights of stairs to the lobby. She ignored Gino, rounded the elevator housing, and stood before the basement door.

She tugged on the door and finally after a big heave wrenched it open.

She stared down the winding stairs where the light disappeared into the heavy, cold dampness. Rose didn't like basements, and she particularly didn't like that basement because she knew Ben lived there. Unfortunately, Ben was the person she wanted to see.

The stairs creaked and Rose wondered if Ben used them like an early warning system, whether he had sensors in each dark corner of the basement, like an animal who has grown into his tunnel, like a mole or gopher.

There was a little red light near the elevator housing and a light in the washroom and other lights scattered through the basement, but they increased the sub-earthly gloom.

The elevator startled her. She watched the cables swinging and wondered again what she was doing there. Rose walked through one cone of light, then stopped inside the second before a door. A few years ago she would never have walked down the steps into the basement, never walked over to Ben's door. It wasn't just Ben; it was anybody. Rose had noticed how her stance towards the world, one which had always been—how exactly had it been?—perhaps deferential was the word, had changed. She was a bookkeeper, a person who tallied and subtracted the fruits of others' labors. She was, she told Mary Reilly, a friend who had died that year, a cipher, perhaps a nonentity. She deferred, she crawled, she was humble, until she started her project. The idea of leaving, of asking people about it, of looking for a helper made her alive. What a riddle! Leaving—the big L—had wiped all that bowing and scraping and deferring right out of her system. She was leaving. What did she care about or whom?

Rose pounded on Ben's door.

There was the sound of boards creaking then an eye in a crack.

"What?!"

"Ben, open up. I want to talk to you."

"Why?"

"Come on. It will only take a minute."

Rose heard a bolt, then a key, then the door opened and she saw Ben muffled up to his head in his long army coat, the coat he wore all year, illuminated in light from a lamp which touched the edges of a thousand tattered books, a bed, and a small gas stove.

Was he the philosopher she'd been seeking?

"Go ahead, ask me in."

Ben cocked his head at her, then shook it as if someone had changed the rules of a cosmic game, croaked out what she took for a laugh, and waved her in with an arm of his coat the hand of which was retracted deep into the sleeve.

There were two chairs embedded in the books, and she walked over and sat in one. She still observed decorum and etiquette, but the big L was close and the niceties of existence fading away. "Ben, do you know what I want to do?" she said abruptly, cutting out the woulds, coulds, and mights, which had larded her speech lately when she'd talked up her project.

"You want to disturb me! I can see that. But you've changed, I can see that too. Well now that you've got me here, I might as well hear it. What do you have to say? Out with it!"

"Don't you use that tone with me, you, you hermit!" Rose caught herself. "I'm sorry for being testy, but I have a very important project. Do you know about it?"

"You want to check out...die. What about it?"

"We prefer 'leaving.' I knew you'd understand."

"Means the same. Life is pain and suffering, death nothing. Take your pick."

"Suffering or nothing; have I gotten too tired, Ben?"

Would it be better to live like Ben, not seeing anyone, knowing where all his books were, connecting to the few things of his existence, than pretending? That's what she felt during all those years in the clothing district counting fancy blouses and skirts and hats and gloves, that she was pretending, that it was a big game, a game where she'd been assigned a position which wouldn't change, which couldn't change, but where somewhere inside, deep within, she knew that it was all pretense, that she was tugging and fussing over the decorations of some elaborate front. She'd been perfect; she'd fit seamlessly into her assigned position so that none of the cracks showed. Except one day she realized it was so false she could scream.

Was leaving the answer? Wasn't there some way of going along which would let her live and cushion the knowledge that she didn't believe anymore, that she'd played that falsehood on herself? Could there be some accommodation?

"Tea?"

He'd offered her tea! "Please. Thanks."

It made her happy that Ben had invited her to tea. She didn't know why. She watched him as he filled an old kettle with water, measured out tea into a tea ball, lighted his little stove with a match, and put the kettle on. Such a curious man, wizened, burr-cut, floppy old WWII coat, a Dickensian turtle who fit into his skin, his carapace, who had lived so long he knew everything.

She knew that was what she needed, not to talk to the Quincys and Rudis and Harrys—those normal people who had done what she'd done—but to talk to someone who had refused to play the game in the same way she had finally refused.

Or was it too late?

The steam from the tea had a wonderful, calm effect on her. She took a few sips, then cradled the mug in her hands. She said, "I've lead a horrible life, counting for other people, trying to understand what my father did, pretending I was happy, or at least adjusted—"

"Those are all other people, other people. Don't care about them."

"I suppose not. I suppose that's the problem. I cared too much about them. But now that I don't have that, what do I have?"

Ben looked at her and shook his head. "You're not ready. You're too alive."

"It's a riddle. Ever since I started the leaving project, I've felt more alive. If I quit my project, I'll go right back to being depressed about everything."

Ben sipped his tea and set the chipped mug down on a bookshelf, leaning towards the door. "It's either/or. Either you live with lies, or don't."

"There's no middle way?"

Ben watched and looked past her, as if he were consulting an oracle. "Maybe."

"What?"

Ben rasped, "The Steppenwolf decided to kill himself at fifty. But instead he went into a bar, found a girl, found love, and found the Magic Theatre. The Magic Theatre was an emanation from his mind, a miasma where he could try killing, love, and reach for the immortals. He failed because he never learned to laugh at his plight, or at himself." Ben pursed his lips, worried. "I suppose I haven't either. The Magic Theatre was a trial." Ben looked up at her, rocked his head slowly from side to side, then looked at her directly. "That's what you need: a trial. Get everything ready, go through the motions, and see what it feels like the next day. See if you want to go through it again, or the real thing."

Rose frowned. "That's not bad," she said. "Not bad at all."

Rose put the mug on a bookshelf towards the back of the room. She got up.

At the door, she turned and said, "Thanks for the tea."

* * *

Rose Tutwiler prepared herself.

She looked at herself in the mirror wondering what had happened. She saw a new edge of determination in her brown eyes, a hard edge to the jaw which was lightly covered with gray hair. She knew exactly what she wanted to do.

First she would put on her robe and go to the elevator—the hallway would be empty if it was still at Christmas. A few minutes later, she would knock on her helper's door. Her helper might be Frieda.

She'd say, "I was wondering if...if you would like to have a glass of port. It's so grim at Christmas. Everyone's gone, the hallways are deserted, it's cold, windy, and..."

Frieda would look at her and, for the first time, Rose saw that Frieda understood what she meant, what she really meant. She would talk about leaving, again, and then about needing a helper and how she couldn't tolerate it anymore. Frieda would listen and nod. Then she left, took the elevator, wondering if it would be her last trip, realizing she hated the elevator: it was red and vile, but familiar; on last trips, even the despicable had a certain charm. The big question was whether her helper would come or not. Would Frieda understand what a "helper" was?

Rose went to the door, opened it, and said to the empty hallway, "Thanks for coming."

Rose closed the door.

Rose pointed to the hiding place of the small brown bottles. She explained exactly what she wanted to do and what she wanted her helper to do.

Rose found two glasses and filled both with Christian Brothers tawny port. She filled another glass with water. She took down an empty pill bottle.

She smiled and held the glass with the water—it seemed heavy, important; she was doing something significant, something she'd dreamed about, something she'd worked for. She looked at the glass one more time, then at her phantom helper, and drank the water as fast as she could.

Done!

She drank deep of the tawny port then held her glass of port up to the light. It was a kaleidoscope of amber lights—the Olympia and Giltmore crimson palaces, NYU high-rise a soft brown tree in a city forest. She coveted the soft buildings as if they were old friends. The noises of sirens had ceased, and a low wind whistled in a strange silence across the city, a chill wind of cleanliness. She turned and appealed to the dark eyes sitting across from her looking out the same window. For the first time in her life she was at one with another being; it was spiritual, something she'd never had with the church.

She drained her glass and put it down, placed the glass on the other side of the table, and put the full glass on her side. She tasted the port.

Now what?

Rose frowned. She should embrace her helper. Rose got up and embraced her phantom helper. She washed her face and walked slowly over to her bed. She took off her robe as if she were about to perform a ceremony. She glanced at the scene near the window and arranged herself in bed, careful to make the seam straight across her breast, her arms resting on the cover.

She was close.

Slam! A strong brown hand closed and locked the door, and rested on the steering wheel, as if getting ready for a long ride.

She felt drowsy, and her room softened and faded. He'd take her to... the races...that nice woman, not like her mother...

Frieda would touch her hair and take her hand and press it. Rose felt peaceful for the first time in her life. She could think and understand without having to do it again, the next day.

She looked at the flickering shadows with her right eye, and struggling slightly, she managed to bring her eye up so she saw the window. There was the dark reflection of her helper over her bed, and beyond she saw the checkerboard lights in the Olympia and, as she became faint, she tried to imagine what the river looked like, that little gray ribbon; but instead, she saw a distant red light flicker on in the Giltmore and that strange green light in the NYU high-rise go out.

The keys dangled from the ignition, that keychain her mother hated, dangling...her father's brown hand turning, the car coming to life.

Then there was darkness and sleep.

The dark figure would smooth out the covers and wait until the pulse drifted away, then tuck her in, one last time. She would seem happy, transformed.

Frieda would reach out and stroke her hair and contemplate her as if Rose had been a problem that had just been solved. Then the shadow would flicker across the wall, loom against the closet door, and stoop to retrieve the empty second glass of port from the window ledge, but stop, almost as if it left Rose's glass too alone. The shadow traced itself more sharply on the wall and stared out the window seeming to wonder what Rose had seen in the drafty red and green high-rises. Finally, the shadow would go to the door. Then, waiting until the hallway was silent and glancing once more at the peaceful Rose, slip out the door leaving it cracked so that she could be discovered later that night, or early in the morning.

* * *

Rose opened her eyes. It was sunny.

She'd gone through her first trial! She was not beholden to anyone. This was the most important thing she would ever do.

She canvassed the room. She saw the candle wax spread over the table, the two glasses, one empty, the other half-full of port.

"No, no. Not right. The glasses have to be empty, the candles have to be bigger, and these covers are too wrinkled. I'm going to need more trials, a lot more trials…and I'm going to need a helper who really helps. I'll write everything down so they get it right."

# Gino

Whenever he worked the desk, he ran out of butts.

Gino probed for a cigarette in the drawer. Instead of a cigarette he touched the club. It was a strange club with soft green plastic on the outside like Teflon, but it was heavy, like it was filled with lead. He liked to feel the bumps on the outside; it reminded him of the club Conan used in one of his sword-and-sorcery tales—it had little bumps on it, like it was carved around the knots in a plastic stump. You could kill somebody with a club like that.

Gino flipped the club up and hit the underside of the desk.

*Thunk. Thunk.*

It made a pleasing, hard sound. Gino knew he shouldn't. He'd argued with his better self about being easier on people. And maybe, he'd thought that before, working at the desk made him do it, made him angry and less accommodating.

He gave in. He made a hit list.

*Thunk. Thunk. Thunk.*

Raymond Butler.

Raymond Butler lived on his own list. He hated Raymond Butler from the day he moved into Ric's room. Poor Ric. They used to talk and drink in the Moat. But in the end, Gino realized, his thing with the CIA got him. It was almost as if the CIA *did* get him. That worm of paranoia ate out of him from inside.

Raymond Butler. He was tall, crew cut, large Adam's apple, pointy head, and stared at people with tiny steel-bearing eyes.

Frank said Raymond had swan-dived over the edge. He worked the desk that day, and he went up to three to reason with Raymond.

Raymond paced his room, agitated like a tin soldier, long arms out, legs stiff, steel eyes boring through some spot on the yellow wall. It was early fall, the chill starting, the leaves falling. The light out Raymond's window was cold. Raymond almost walked into the wall, but then he'd stop and swivel around like he was a mechanical man, or R2-D2 who had popped a circuit. Gino had tried reason, then he said he'd call the cops. Raymond stopped, drew up his long, lean frame, and his eyes got tiny and mean and he'd called him a fat alkie and come at him. Gino had liked that. He'd wanted to fuck him up, but Raymond had turned on his heel at the last second, and he'd followed his punch to the floor and broken his hand. Frieda had taken him to the hospital.

Of course, he told everybody that Raymond had tried to hit him.

*Thunk. Thunk.*

Mildred...and George.

*Thunk, thunk.*

Mildred yelled at him—again, last night—about the boom-box in 711. And George. Gino knew it was George because he always heard George's thin whistle, then he heard George's whisper. He knew George had sucked a quick breath of oxygen from the green bottle. "Fucking toilet...fucking toilet...I hate that fuuu..." Then George's scratchy voice got softer and died out.

*Thunk. Thunk. Thunk.*

Time to expand the hate. Feel the hate. What about things? There was the boiler, the elevator—he'd need bombs for those. The telephone: he could demolish the telephone with that club—he'd put a wastebasket over it last night and let it ring for hours.

*Thunk. Thunk. Thunk.*

When Gino worked himself up, he dreamed of walking through the Rex and taking care of everyone and everything that made his life miserable: the Mildreds, Raymonds, Georges...the telephone.

Gino sat back, pleased with his fantasy, put the club back in the drawer, drew the red cap further down over his ears, and adjusted his red scarf so it covered his chins. The red-and-white edge of his crumpled Marlboro pack peeked out of the wastebasket. Gino sighed, looked at the window, the radiator, the TV on the chair, and finally the small space heater glowing a few feet away.

Gino moved the space heater closer.

He stared out the little half-oval at the wall and mused about the stops and starts of the last year. Inevitably, he scratched the mental itch of why he was fifty-three and sitting at the Rex desk. Fired from Nopalito—that's when his life started its latest nosedive.

That's what he told John Farmer a few days earlier in the Moat. It was a ball-shrinking cold, the sun gray in the Moat doorway. At the end of the bar, Fred read a book, and at every page looked up to see if he had any customers.

At least he was inside, a bottle in his hand and someone to talk to, to explain. Gino had felt, without coming out and saying it, that he was under siege. John carefully put his gray hat on the bar, bunched his eyebrows like that old actor, Carradine, and leaned towards him.

"Ya know it comes down to that fuckin' job every time," he'd said, gripping his longneck tightly. Gino finished his scotch, had a small hit of beer. "Sure it was my fault, but it was their fault, too."

John's eyebrows went up a fraction. "Who's 'they'?"

"Those stuck-up assholes—the ones with the blond hair, noses, and freckles. They all look alike. They look at you like you're slime mold and pretend they're pissed at summmpin', or they're really this or really that— they can't live without that fuckin' word. I think it's because they're not *really* anything. This guy says his fuckin' linguine ain't done. Well, I says, ain't that too bad. Ya know how you tell if it's done, I says. You throw it on the wall, like this. Just missed the manager, standin' like a sore head near the kitchen. Didn't even get that last check—fuckin' said it was for damages."

John laughed and shook his head, although he'd heard it before. "We've been colonized and settled—we might as well admit it." John shook his head and looked at his beer. "But at least you're a free man— you do what you want."

"With no money that ain't a lot. Fifty-three and stuck at the desk. Course there are worse things. Just can't think of them right now."

John said, "Melissa said the other day—you know I hate to admit she's right about anything because she's usually wrong, or at least aggravating. She said that we're being squeezed from both sides—if it's not the yuppies, it's the crazies. Look at the third floor: two years ago it was clean, everybody was happy...or at least they tolerated one another— Melissa has never been exactly happy. Look at the floor now. First, we get the messengers, then the roaches, then Ric dies, then we get Raymond Butler. What the fuck is going to happen next?"

"Bannon's—gone; that place was an institution."

"Bannon's was gone years ago. I guess Plato's is next. I heard...let's not talk about it."

"Who fuckin' knows? Who fuckin' knows? All I know is that they took over Nopalito and I got fired. I never got fired before...maybe it is me. You reach a point you don't want to take crap anymore."

"Gino, you're one of the last of the Real People. You deserve a nightcap." He was happy for the free drink, but it was a bribe so John could complain about Melissa.

Gino remembered he wanted a cigarette, and his fingers dug through the wastebasket for a butt he'd thrown out last night. When he slept and let it burn, most of the butt was still there. Gino found one, evened it out, squeezed the ashes off between his thumb and forefinger. He contemplated his past in the diaphanous haze obscuring the lobby.

Maybe he was on the slide down. He'd thought it before, but not seriously. You always think you're on the way up...or at least in a holding zone waiting for the next uptick.

The problem with the desk was that it encouraged his worst habits, the downtick. He watched soaps on the tiny TV, which worked if you hung the antenna just right over the radiator, ate—that took a lot of time—smoked, and slept. His only real exercise was screaming into the phone at Mildred or George or the Raymond Butlers who made his winter at the desk miserable. And he snuck in his bottle. Those nights slipped through his week like cracked mirrors. Last week, loaded, he went to his room and slept for two hours. Rudi said he'd fire him if he did it again.

Downtick, or waiting for the uptick. Just like the stockbrokers.

Gino felt the heat against his fingers, took a last puff and mashed the butt into the blackened brass ashtray. Harry said his liver was going, and if that didn't get him, his lungs would. He'd had the tests at Bellevue before he was fired. Harry was right. He had to knock off booze and butts, or they'd knock him off. But it was the image of pushing around a little bottle of oxygen and whispering at people that made him try to clean up his act. He did try. He chewed Nicorettes and drank weak light beers, but it was hardly the same. The light beer made him bloated, like a puff-fish he'd seen on Nature, and the Nicorettes gave him indigestion. Together they gave him a shitty copy of a good time, not the good time itself. He missed the heat. He went back to butts and whiskey.

On the way down. Downtick. He didn't like to think about it, but it was there. On the one hand, he had a good rep; on a good day, he did a fifth. Everybody talked about it.

He knew that was wrong too. It was part of the syndrome. And he knew, secretly, or sometimes when he had these talks with himself, that he was seriously on the Downtick.

Whenever he felt like that, there was one thing that helped: a party. He was gregarious and had lots of parties. Gino thought about the last party. They sat on his bed or in his chairs and talked and got plastered. It was like Mario's Circle on seven, except Mario's was more exclusive.

The best time for a party was at five. He'd open his door, sit in his best chair in the corner, prop his short legs on the bed and have the first couple of drinks before the guests arrived. He'd watch the doors opening and closing on the east side of the hall and yell to everybody who passed. When Kurt came to his first party, Kurt told him he was like Cerberus, a three-headed dog guarding the Gates of Hell. Sergei said he was a fat little Petrushka who scuttled around their personal block in Moscow pretending to sweep but watching people come and go and reporting on what they were doing, like a spy. He couldn't explain it. It was the best time, those moments watching people come and go. People-watching, they call it.

He found another half-smoked butt. He was trying to even it out when the elevator cranked up. He swiveled and watched the red door. A few seconds later a tall form in gold-frame German glasses and a soft lined leather coat walked into the lobby.

"Hey, Eric. What youse doin' up? It's too fuckin' cold to be up this early."

"Gotta meet somebody."

"Eric, do me a favor. Come here."

"Haven't time. I've got to meet him in twenty minutes."

Gino wasn't going to ask who he'd meet at six on Thursday morning.

"Eric, I'm out of butts. Could ya get me a pack? Please. And a regular with tree sugars. You know, the Korean place."

"If they're not busy. Sometimes they have lines early in the morning."

"Hookers from midtown—that's funny. Imagine being a hooker in weather like this."

"That's going to be in a play some day—they're natural characters. There's so much—"

"Eric, I'd appreciate it." Eric looked at Gino as if he were thinking about something else, nodded as if it were only a mild imposition and took the stack of change that Gino had arranged on the counter. Eric opened the door and slipped into the darkness.

Eric came back a few minutes later with butts and steaming coffee.

Gino got very warm. "Youse got to be careful, Eric. Youse got to stay away from things. Know what I mean?"

Eric looked at Gino as if he were judging what to say. He leaned into the half-oval and rested his elbow on the ledge. Eric shrugged. "It's a rite of passage, Gino." Gino nodded, but he didn't see. "An obligation of great writers...a necessity. You see, I have the talent. I have the words and I have the structure. But I don't have enough material. You have to have material! It has to come from somewhere!" Eric shook his head and sighed. He ran long fingers through his hair. His hair settled slowly back over his glasses.

Gino nodded his head in sympathy. "Writing is tough—it stopped me in the second grade! Listen, Eric. Tonight, or tomorrow—make it tomorrow; come over and have a drink. I'm inviting everybody on our floor—and some other floors. I'm gonna have a little party. My door is open, anyway. If you're not doing anything."

"Sure—who's coming?"

"A lot of people. Fuck, you'll know; you live right acrost from me!"

"Sure, sure." Eric looked at the brown desk and seemed unsure about leaving its security. "I'll be over, but now I have to go."

"I appreciate, believe me. Thanks for the smokes and coffee."

Gino waited for the door to slam and then settled into a nice smoke and hot coffee. Gino watched the smoke spread through the lobby and thought of his changing attitude towards Eric. He'd hated him when he moved in across from him—he told Rudi he didn't like it. But Gino saw he wasn't bad for being a fag and starting to mess with drugs—he hated to see that start. He told John that it was funny, how under the surface, Eric had the same problems as everybody else.

\* \* \*

A new front moved in, white swirls roamed like ghosts through Central Park, and street people huddled on benches in Union Square.

Wisps of snow circled the Rex's bare steps; bone-chilling cold kept the residents in. Most felt the pleasant limbo of Friday afternoon.

Gino felt the release too, even though he had to work the desk Saturday and Sunday. He bought a couple extra bottles of Old Grand-Dad, some beer, a couple of Pepsis and Seven-ups for the sissies, potato chips, onion dip, French bread, and soft cheese. He put everything except the booze on a large serving tray on the little table against the wall, which left a foot between the table and his bed, but it was enough to squeeze by. The booze he kept in a rack at the bottom of his bed and dispensed like a bartender at an open bar.

Gino looked admiringly at his room. Most people in the Rex didn't know how to live or how to do a room. The bead curtain hiding the alcove was a nice touch, and so was the soft chair with little tassels next to the window and the red silky Chinese lantern hanging from the window. That was from the Chinese New Year ten years ago! Gino was amazed it had been that long. He'd built a pine board shelf over his bed for his library. He had a couple pots of philodendra up there, a thick stack of *Boobs on Broadway*, and a hundred—he counted them once—sword-and-sorcery novels. He liked Robert Howard best, and late at night, after he'd put down a Conan adventure, he was Gino the iron-thewed barbarian rescuing the Ice Queen from the steely grip of her brothers, the frost giants.

But the artistic centerpiece of his room was a poster over the little table. It was a dreamy painting of a winding path through a flower garden by Monet. It stared at him from the back of the Salvation Army on Broadway a couple of years ago. Cost him three bucks, but it gave the place class. Luce told him it was Monet's garden at Give-Ernie. Sometimes, just before he was about to pass out, he'd look at it and he could swear the flowers moved! Frieda said it was partly the booze and partly because it was painted like a photo out of focus.

His room was cozy. The chair in the corner was large, the bed covered with a down comforter, rimmed with soft pillows.

Gino put on a clean white t-shirt, dark lightweight sports coat for his butts and lighter, and his best shorts. Then, approving of how he looked, made himself a whiskey and soda in his favorite cut-glass tumbler and did the Cerberus routine. He forgot the drafty nights at the desk as he watched residents open and close doors, listened to the stray shout and the elevator grinding through the floors.

Gino reached a balance he always reached with his first drink. Everything seemed right; everything was right in its place. Didn't matter that he had no real job or no real money. At least he had whiskey. That's the problem, he thought, with all those people trying to reform him. It might not be good for him, but he liked it. You have to like something.

Eric came home and Gino yelled across the carpet that he had to come over. Jimmy, the recluse at the end of the hall, came by and Gino yelled at him. But Jimmy just lowered his head and walked in that slow shuffle. George pushed his oxygen up to his door and stopped to look at him. Gino pretended to be looking somewhere else, but he heard George's thin whistle and saw him shake his head out of the corner of his eye, turn, and push his bottle back towards his room.

Mary came, appearing in the doorway like a thick red stump with steel-bristle hair.

Mary said, "A party? Where'd ya get the money?"

"Hey, beautiful. Have a drink." Mary took some Grand-Dad and sat on the corner of Gino's bed. Gino smiled and his eyelids lowered. "How ya feel? Ya feel like playin' a little? We got the time. I could close the door."

Mary shook her head, brayed. "Are you kiddin'? I got a guy. I tole you."

Gino looked puzzled. "Where did this guy come from?"

"I tole you once, and I won't tell you again. Besides it's private. Didn't the doc tell you to cut the booze?"

"I tried—a month ago, I tole ya."

"I remember—pissy beer and gum. No wonder you went back."

Gino's eyelids lowered again. "You're lookin' good anyway."

"You're sure subtle. But I got a guy who could cut you in half."

He hated Mary when she pulled tough stuff. "Alex is comin' later. Youse can say hello."

"She just better keep out of my way."

Gino didn't like Alex either. He wasn't sure what she was doing at the Rex. Nobody actually *planned* to be at the Rex. "Youse can tell her yerself. She's comin' in ten minutes. She ast special about ya."

Mary got up. "Screw her. Did you invite everybody you ever knew?"

Gino looked astounded, innocent. He looked into amber liquid in his glass and the melting ice cubes and said, "Leavin' so early?"

"Got to see my boyfriend."

"I'll tell Alex you ast after her. C'mon, stay around."

Mary shot him a dirty look, left the empty glass on the small table, and left.

"Give your new boyfriend my regards."

Gino chuckled. He was glad Mary left...and he was glad he got in that dig about Alex. He debated whether to ask her. She irritated people, but he did want people, a lot of people.

Gino heaved off the bed and walked to the hall phone and had Rudi patch him through to Alex. "Hey, come on up. There'll be lots of people you can talk to."

Alex said she might.

Gino got back just as Eric opened his door. There was a spill that ran from Gino's door to Eric's. Gino thought he'd done it when that Brit lived across the hall. Her name was Maggie, and she only lived there two weeks, but she liked to drink and came over every night. She gave him her plants when she left—"in memoriam," she said—and the philodendron still curled around his bookshelf, and the fern sprayed up towards the Chinese lantern.

Eric sat on the bed near Gino. "You're becoming an institution, Gino."

"Eric, Eric. What am I going to do with youse? Have a drink." Gino poured Eric two fingers of whiskey.

"I can't drink all this."

"Eric, let me tell ya something." Gino leaned over and, grasping Eric's shoulder with his soft hand, whispered confidentially. "I know what you're doin' and youse gotta stop, ya know? You're hurtin' yourself wit them drugs, you're hurtin' yourself bad."

"What about booze? I hear your liver's losing."

"I know, I know, Eric. It's my curse—this fuckin' stuff. But you're young. It's hard fer me ta see that in somebody like you." Gino shook his head and wiped a mock tear from his face. "Don't go no place; I got plenty of people comin'.

"I'll stay awhile."

Brucie and Sven appeared in the door at the same time. Gino said, "I got to do the honors."

Brucie stood near the door. His eyes seemed to rotate as they took in the room. He said, "Fucking Yankees." Listening to Brucie was an obligation—if you knew him—you just didn't want to listen very long.

Gino poured Brucie a drink. Brucie edged by the table, took the drink and sat in the chair near the window. Sven had his own beer and sat on the bed near the door.

The long quizzical form of John Farmer framed the doorway in back of Brucie, looking happier than he usually looked when he was with his wife.

After Gino did the honors with John, he turned back to Brucie.

"What did the Yankees do this time—lose? They're always losin'. Ya got to come up with sumpin' new, Brucie. I got it—why don't youse follow anudder team—it's simple." Brucie looked at Gino like he had just told him to murder his mother. "Or anudder sport like polo!"

"There's only one sport and only one team, and that's baseball and the Yankees. Once there was the Dodgers and the Giants, but they're traitors."

"They're like an institution—like Gino's parties."

"The Yankees are a real institution. What's going to happen to your parties when Gino croaks? Tell me that?"

"Hey, wait a minute—it ain't baseball season. It's the middle of the fucking winter. What the fuck's wrong with the Yankees now? Don't they get any peace?"

"Trades, getting ready for spring training...I don't like it!"

Gino said, "Good, let's not talk about them. Who's this guy Mary's got?"

"I don't gossip; besides I told you the other day."

"That's all youse do. What else is there ta do, sittin' on the front steps like a gargoyle."

Brucie shook his head, laughed. "Some guy, that's all. We know he isn't good looking, and he can't have much money."

"That's not very nice, Brucie."

Brucie shrugged. "She's not very nice—Mary is Mary."

"Mary skipped like a rabbit when I tole her Alex was gonna stop up."

Eric bit his lower lip with his teeth. "Alex? When's she coming?"

"Sometime soon; I can call."

Eric shrugged. "She'll either come or not."

"Sven, you ever meet Eric? Sven is the artist on the tenth floor. He's good too; be nice."

Eric turned to the thin white-haired man sitting next to him. Sven had been watching and smiling to himself. When Eric nodded at him, Sven looked at him and said, "You're the writer?"

"How did you know?"

Sven waved at Gino and Brucie. "The Rex grapevine."

"Don't stultify my reputation," said Gino. Gino took a long pull of his drink; then his body settled into the bed.

"I'm writing a play," said Eric, finally.

"Can you talk about it?"

Eric relaxed, took a quick hit of whiskey, and gestured with his hands. "It's called *Fall from the Top*. It's full of intrigue, sub-plots, exotic characters—Fallon, a miserly old man, paranoid tycoons, moguls, the struggle for a doomed factory. The factory is a metaphor for their wasted lives. The mogul has a brilliant son, Eugene, who is a playwright—so far, he's my best character—and there's Orlando." Eric glanced at Gino and shook his head. "He's supposed to kidnap Eugene, but the character isn't working out."

Sven said, "Do you know many tycoons, moguls, and kidnappers?"

Eric frowned, then said, "The characters are props and, as for the background, everyone knows about money and violence in America— it's our heritage. What's important is the structure—I call it the map, or the Master Plan...and the playwright—Eugene. Once the map is right, and Eugene is fleshed out, the play writes itself."

"Maps, playwrights within plays. It's complicated."

Eric smiled. "It mirrors our society—it's a microcosm, and the play-wright is the center, the interpreter, the key."

"I have a weakness for simplicity—simple and small, and I've been forced inside."

"This weather—"

"Not weather, ambience. The new people in the neighborhood, the gentrification. The interesting people chased out, or chased in here. The Rex is a wildlife refuge or fragile ecosystem under siege."

"There are a lot of characters here." Eric looked at Gino again and ran his hand through his hair, and it settled slowly over the gold rims of his glasses. He looked around as if he were wondering when he could leave.

"This is one of mine." Sven touched a miniature portrait of Gino but then picked another from off the bookshelf from behind the philodendron and handed it to Eric. "There are a few scattered through the Rex—I call it my lending gallery, but most are upstairs." The little painting showed glasses, a wave of salt-and-pepper hair, an animated troubled face. It was flat, almost child-like, but the expression on Rudi's face wasn't that of a child.

Eric held the small portrait in his hand and turned it to the light in the hall, as if he were trying to find its hidden value. "Good art must have..." Eric paused and looked at Sven as if he didn't want to insult him. "...control, distance."

Sven took the portrait back, held it in his large bony hand, and looked at it critically. "You don't like it. That's all right; most people don't, but I never wanted to be liked."

Eric twirled his fraternity ring around his finger, took it off, and made a cameo of a small bald man who had appeared in the doorway. He rubbed it on his sweater, slipped it on his finger, and turned back to Sven. "You have a plain style."

"When I was younger, I was attracted to Die Brücke, the revival of the woodcut form. It forces you to concentrate on what is important. I still use flat colors that don't draw attention to themselves—that don't detract from expression. This portrait of Rudi, for example. You see the glasses, the sunken eyes, the hair. He is recognizable. But what's interesting for me is the eyes and mouth—expression. Rudi's eyes are soft, hurt; they want to cry. But the mouth is small, rounded, pinched, as if he's seen too much to cry."

"There's a place for all art—operas and operettas, Picasso and—"

"My poor little painting." Sven laughed. He picked his words deliberately, as if he were wondering out loud. "Isn't character the most important thing?"

"Playwrights work with characters, not character."

Sven smiled and watched Gino and John Farmer while he spoke. "You need both, but the surface should show the soul. By itself, it never holds my attention very long." Sven put the portrait back on the shelf, next to the cover of a fantasy hero with smoldering blue eyes.

Eric looked at Sven. He seemed old—his legs were thin, dry, and bare because of the heat which rattled the steam pipes. His hands were brown with dark spots, his fingers long and knobby but tentative. There were crisscrossed lines on his face and a burst of white hair. But his eyes were mischievous, a curious amalgam of seriousness and irony.

"How big is your gallery?"

"Come up. I may even do your portrait. I have portraits of most people who live here."  "I'd like a good portrait."

"It depends what you mean by 'good.' Sometimes, I think my hand has become too independent. It goes for the soul, pain."

Eric twirled his ring. "Have you suffered?"

"Once." Sven looked at Eric as if he were looking beyond the words, weighing the hint of a sneer that tugged at the corner of Eric's mouth. "I painted my pain, once, but I stopped."

"The artist's pain is the only pain."

"Ah. The old struggle between the mirror and the door."

"Door?"

"The longer you stare in the mirror, the less you see."

Gino turned on the bed and looked at Sven and Eric. "Youse guys are gabbin' a lot. Whats youse talkin' about?"

"A little painting."

Gino laughed and reached for a new bottle. "I tole ya he was good, didn't I?"

* * *

Gino was drunk when Alex got there.

"Hey babe...Alex, tanks for droppin' by. Eric! Eric! Alex's here!"

Alex nodded at Brucie and John Farmer and greeted the other people scattered in pockets around Gino's soft room, talked to Gino for a minute, and poured her own glass of whiskey. She sipped the whiskey, glanced at Eric's open door and saw Eric watching her from the big chair with the shiny tacks behind his bed.

Alex sauntered across the carpet to Eric's room. Eric's room was a tiny palace: shiny brass bed and lamp, a dark bookcase, the leather chair, a director's chair, and a table with a typewriter at the window. Roman ruins—a Piranesi poster—on the wall above the bed hinted at a wider world.

Alex sat in the director's chair, and Eric posed in the corner, feet propped on the brass bed-frame looking preppie in sweater, cords, and polished penny loafers. He had a new reddish beard, and his fine hair spread over thin gold glasses and his left eye. His mouth was spoiled, fatuous, set. He looked like a porcelain figurine, Camille in a schlock shop—artificial, hokey, glazed.

Gino heard:

"...ah the Big Adventure."

"...it should have been easier."

"...'Life at the Top of the Bottom,' by Eric."

"...You don't have say anything."

Gino didn't remember much after that. Sometimes he zoned out—he knew that. The next thing he knew Alex was back.

Gino turned to her. "Alex...Alex. Have annudder little hit." Gino was propped up in his TV viewer, a glass of booze in his puffy hand, his legs splayed, topped by tiny leather slippers. Gino looked tired, heavy, but he surveyed the remains of his party like a king. He grabbed a half bottle of Grand-Dad at the end of the bed and poured her some whiskey.

"Gino, are you OK? You don't look so good."

"Yeah, end of the night, I always look the same. Probably have a hangover tomorrow. And fuck, I have to work."

Alex sat on the bed and watched him. "How long do you think you can do this?"

Gino, surprised, slurred, "What?"

"Drink and smoke?"

"Dat's what everbody says. Dat's what Harry says. But ain't everbody gonna die?"

"Ever ask yourself why you drink?"

"Huh?"

Alex smiled sardonically "There's always a reason. Too short, too ugly, no girls, not smart enough. There's always a reason."

Gino said, "Right now, I don't care. Know what I mean? And why do youse care?"

"It's important people know who they are."

"Maybe I don't care. Maybe I like what I do."

Alex got up. "Enjoy that whiskey. It might be your last."

* * *

Where did everyone go?

It happened too often lately. He was like the Blarney Stone—a place to touch base, but never a place to stay. He never moved, and he hadn't moved for a long time. Most of the time, he liked that. He could look at his Monet and dream about the colors or mix his sword-and-sorcery collection with Monet's color. It was the colors again. Never affected him like that before. But that night he felt like company. He wasn't feeling good. And when you didn't feel good, you wanted company.

Anyone but Alex.

Raymond Butler walked stiffly by.

Gino waited a beat, then said, "Raymond."

He knew Raymond wouldn't stop, but he didn't hear steps.

Raymond edged back into view. Raymond stared at him the way he'd stared when he broke his hand.

Gino didn't know what to say. Why had he said anything? He wasn't going to ask Raymond what he was doing on the wrong floor. "Wanna drink?"

Raymond was puzzled. He looked back down the hall; then he looked back. "Why?"

Gino shrugged. Damn good question. Why? He wasn't sure he could answer that question without telling the truth...which was that he was lonely. You didn't admit that kind of thing to anyone. Gino Valerio especially didn't admit that kind of thing to Raymond Butler, resident psycho.

"I just want somebody to talk to."

"And anybody will do?"

96

Gino got pissed, because it was too close to the truth. "You're the last person—"

"What you got?"

What had he done? He didn't want to talk to Raymond. But he'd backed himself into being a host. That was the one thing he did okay. Of course, you needed more than a Raymond Butler to be a real host.

Groans of the building. The elevator. A distant voice rising slightly and falling. He'd heard those sounds for years. He hated to admit it, but they were a comfort. He hated the cold, and he hated the desk. His room was okay. It was home. He had his sword-and-sorcery collection, his booze, the fridge, his Monet. Gino edged deeper into his stuffed chair.

"Whiskey. But tell me, Raymond. Are you supposed to drink?"

"Why not?"

"You know, with the meds."

Raymond's steely eyes narrowed. His tongue flicked out of his long face and ran around his lips, as if thinking about leaving. He'd edged into the room, and now he seemed to be edging out. His shoulders hitched up then relaxed. "How do you know about the meds?"

"Shit, Raymond, you tell everyone."

"I suppose I do. Yeah, booze is okay. They told me not to get another addiction, something I would be obsessive about. That's part of the problem."

"Shit we all have that. Things we can't give up. Like me and booze and the butts."

"Yeah."

"Sit on the bed, Raymond. Might as well be comfortable." Raymond shrugged and then propped his hip on the side of the bed. "Listen, Ray, know what?" Raymond shook his head. "If everybody hated the things they liked, we wouldn't be compulsive about anything."

"I don't like booze, but I don't mind it. A small one."

Gino picked out a wine glass, poured an inch of whiskey in it, and handed it to Raymond.

Raymond said, "Wine glass?"

Gino titled his head towards Raymond. "It ain't the Ritz, Ray."

Ray laughed. "For sure." Raymond looked around the room, then out the open door.

"So why do you take these meds, Raymond? If you don't mind my asking. You seem like a reasonable person."

Gino wasn't sure what he was saying. He was actually asking Raymond about his life. Everyone knew Raymond was a whacko, out-to-lunch, a couple cans short of a six-pack, and irritating. Yesterday, he wanted to crush his skull with a lead-weighted green club.

"They say I have some kind of affective disorder, bipolar. I don't remember anymore. I get hyper, then I get depressed. It adds up to crazy." Raymond's Adam's apple bounced up, then down. He waved his hand. "I just take the stuff."

They might not be so far wrong, thought Gino, but he was curious. "What do you think? You think you're crazy? You know a lot of artists are crazy. Or do drugs." Gino thought of Eric and his early morning "meeting." Drugs. Everybody took 'em. He took 'em too.

"I'm no artist."

"You don't have to be. I meant you were in good company."

"Most of the time, it doesn't feel like that."

"But you still kinda know what's goin' on?"

"Sometimes I know I'm acting strange. Sometimes I watch myself, as if I'm standing outside watching this strange guy named Raymond who can't stop doing what he's doing."

Gino shrugged and said, "It doesn't matter, does it?"

Raymond looked around again. "You got a nice place here. I don't have much; sometimes I think I could have more."

"I didn't want to say anything, but you ain't got nothin'. You know a bed, a tiny chest, a table, and one chair. You're livin' too much with yourself."

"Maybe. Say, I'm sorry about that hand."

"Wasn't your fault. I got a little too jumpy."

The Rex was a desert that night. It was cold, sure, but didn't people want to stay in and socialize? Where were Mary and Brucie? Instead, he was drinking with Raymond "Crazy Man" Butler. But that's what he had; might as well make the best of it.

Raymond finished his drink and said, "Thanks for the drink."

"Thanks for comin' in. I appreciate it."

* * *

98

Gino, bleary-eyed, anesthetized, surveyed his room.

Potato chips and small glasses of whiskey, soda, and cans of beer were strewn in awkward locations. There was an after-odor of scotch, beer, and grease.

He laughed at a mouse who came out to eat the cheese and crumbs under the table. His little nose twitched; he seemed like a tiny phantom, a messenger from a dark part of the Rex.

Gino felt blasted and watched anger and happiness chase each other in Monet's garden of Give-Ernie. The manager of Nopalito walked down the path and faded into pinks, yellows, and greens.

"Fuckin' job." Gino allowed himself the fantasy of blowing the manager away.

The desk. "Fuckin' desk."

George. George, the snake, had pushed his green bottle into the door around nine and took a hit of oxygen. He knew George was going to talk.

"Fucking noise...fucking noise..."

"Get lost George. Take a hike before I get my club."

"Fucking noise...fuuu..." George's breath leaked out, and he looked at Gino with hate coiled in his eyes.

The party was a success, a big success. He'd been the center, the ringmaster, the iron-thewed Master of Ceremonies.

Even Rudi had come.

Gino shook his head about Rudi. There were low points in the night—Alex, for example. But Rudi was not a high point either. Rudi was like a cop—having a good time was definitely at the bottom of Rudi's list. Rudi told him he was drinking too much, then that everyone was drinking too much, and finally that the neighbors would complain.

Gino had scolded him.

"You have to have a good time sometime—doncha? Christ, you work twelve hours a day and spend an hour on the subway gettin' back ta Queens, and what for?"

"A job and nobody tells me what to do—that's enough for me."

"That's life?" Gino shook his head.

"Life, life—what does anyone in this country know about life? People spend their time not thinking about life. Everything is a distraction: TV, deodorant, booze—you have things—if you got the money. But you can't be different or get sick or old."

"Youse don't have a good life, Rudi."

"Life is more than stuffing yourself," said Rudi sadly. Rudi felt his glasses to make sure they were still on his head, then sighed.

He tried to talk Rudi into having a beer, but Rudi stood at the door and watched everybody and looked sour like he had things on his mind besides having a good time. He drank some soda water, dropped his glasses over his eyes, and left to check an apartment on five.

Raymond Butler. Who would have thought? "Hah...hah..." Gino coughed and felt a little pain in his side.

The gray ghost nibbling on his crackers jerked his nose and disappeared into the corner, and Gino glanced at the underside of his pine shelf.

The new Conan! Conan was old! He had gray hair, a sword, and faced a green dragon with a long red tongue! It was too far to reach, and he was too drunk to read. He looked at the remains of the party, again, and decided to pour himself a nightcap.

He reached the bottle in the rack and emptied the last inch into his glass.

*Thud.*

Gino looked at the bottle lying on its side, a small drop on the lip.

Gino's bald head dropped, then jerked back, and his puffy hand brought the glass up and touched his chin; then he raised it to his mouth. He took a taste, but it dribbled over his chin and wetted his tee-shirt.

The colors swirled in Give-Ernie, faces forming and disappearing... the manager, George, Kurt, Alex. Gino laughed, coughed.

Gino knew he was blasted and lay on his back, and his eyes slowly shut.

The glass balanced on his chest between his soft fingers, like a glass flower on a mound of earth, and followed the rising and falling of Gino's breath with the regularity of a metronome.

The gray ghost sniffed in the shadow cast by Gino's leg, and his whiskers touched Gino's slipper. A sharp pain made Gino shift his bulk; the ghost disappeared. The glass tilted and fell.

The glass rolled on the carpet and stopped.

*　*　*

Frieda and Rudi walked glumly to Bellevue under a cold gray sky.

Rudi said, "No one understands what I do... Ric, Gino. People who are alone."

Frieda said, "This is Gino. It's different."

"Everyone is different."

"Gino should have—"

Rudi sighed. "He thought he would live forever; life never thinks about death. What I hate is the final cleaning...storing clothes, the plastic Jesus of someone who hid herself for sixty years, fixing a broken handle."

Frieda saw Rudi was tired. The sky was oppressive, the short walk long and painful. It was cold, too cold for the roof, but she would have preferred being there any day.

Big ward. The overworked attendant came over and put up a movable partition which gave the illusion of privacy.

Rudi looked worried, kept his glasses in his hair, and stared over the sparse hairs on Gino's head into another world.

Frieda, resigned, tried to appear hopeful, as if optimism would make Gino get better.

The doctor told them Gino didn't have a chance—inoperable liver cancer.

Frieda said, "Some party."

"It will be the last one for a while. I got the idea."

Frieda knew Gino would never get the idea. "You'll have more when you get out."

"Frieda... Frieda, where is everybody?"

"Sven came yesterday."

"Yeah, that's too bad. I was asleep. Eric?"

"He might come later. The others will be here."

"Yeah, sure. Everybody's got a lot to do. Did ya talk ta the doc?"

"Yes." Frieda watched Gino's fingers drumming slowly on the bed, and she saw that Rudi kept his eyes on the folds in the white sheet strung around Gino's bed.

"Not so good."

"No, not so good."

"But ya know somethin'?" Gino's arms were thick on the covers. Frieda heard whispers, as if people were afraid of violating the stillness.

Rudi looked over Gino's head. "What?"

"If I wanted ta, I could beat it. Ya know what I mean? I think that if yer strong enough, ya can beat anything—it's like America right now; we're in this thing about not givin' a fuck, ya know? But you know something?"

"What?"

"I don't wanta beat it. I'm tired. I feel beat. I don't think I'm gonna make it." Gino looked sad, and his soft face seemed to melt, and a tear rolled down his cheek. Frieda felt an immense tiredness, as if she'd been thrust into a role she didn't want and didn't understand.

"You have to fight, Gino."

Rudi ran his fingers over the loose end of his belt. "Everyone has to fight—it's human nature. You'll get better, you stay in the hospital for a while."

Gino looked at her, wondering. "Do me a favor, Frieda."

"Whatever you want."

"Bring me a little bottle and some butts, and my last Conan book."

"But Gino..."

Rudi shook his head. "That would be criminal."

"And tell Mary and the others to visit—I don't want ta die alone. Frieda, please, this one thing—I don't want ta die alone."


Gino slowly opened his eyes. He was lying on his side, and part of the sheet covering his body hid most of the ward. Beyond it was white, white everywhere. The white slowly became shapes, lumps, drawn faces perched on sheets.

He sat up and turned his head. Over the hump of his stomach was a cadaverous figure with steely eyes.

Raymond Butler.

"Raymond, what are you doing here?"

"Heard you were sick. Thought I'd see how you were doing?"

"Thanks. That's nice, that's nice. Ain't been many people stopping by."

"So how are you doing?"

"Not so good Raymond, not so good."

Raymond looked abashed. He stared over Gino's head as if into a strange undiscovered country. "That's too bad."

Gino raised himself up and smoothed the sheets. "You doing okay?"

"Yeah. I'm in one of my even phases. Everything level...not too much up or down."

"Say, Raymond, I've been thinking. It's gonna take me time to get outta here. Why don't you keep that print on the wall for me? You know, safe keeping."

Ray stared. "But it's yours."

"Youse need something in that room; we already talked about it. I'll tell Rudi."

"It's pretty."

"And any of my books you want. Know what, take anything you want. When I get out, I'll take it back."

Raymond frowned, bunching lines on his forehead. "I'll give 'em back."

"No hurry, no hurry."

"Well, I'll see you then. I'll come back tomorrow."

"Thanks Raymond. Thanks a lot. And Ray."

"Yeah."

"Don't forget to take your meds."

"Right."


Rudi rested his head on his hand.

Gino died two days ago. He didn't have any relatives. He opened Gino's room and according to his instructions told people to come up. Mary got his booze, Frieda his plants, and in a strange turn, Gino asked him to give his Monet poster to Raymond Butler. Raymond took it and a few books. Little pieces of Gino everywhere, as if the Rex were an organism absorbing an injured part.

He stored the rest in the basement.

Gino was never the best at the desk, but he was Gino, somebody you could count on to be there. Rudi opened the ledger to Gino's page. The scratches insignificant, smudges, but important in an existential way.

Ben appeared from the side of the elevator housing. He walked slowly into the lobby and stopped in front of Rudi.

"Gino? Hah!" Ben laughed out loud; his laugh was a sharp clap, impotent thunder arcing up from his steel bristles. "When did he die?"

"A couple days ago. Why do you care?"

"Inevitabilities, I suppose."

Rudi knew he shouldn't, but the day before he died, he'd taken a small bottle and the latest Conan book to Gino. He'd seen a pumpkin under a white sheet that looked sad, that didn't want to die in a hospital. Poor Gino. He'd seen him again the last night, when he was unconscious. Gino was not a good worker, but people liked him, and used him. And he was part of what the Rex was about; in a sense he *was* the Rex, the first person you saw when came in, the last person you saw when you went out. A fixture.

Ben's laugh jerked through the lobby. "Everybody used him—hah, hah! Hee, hee, hee!"

Rudi was grim. "What matter is it? Death is death. The only people who have to know are the people with the papers. But why should we know? As if we care about exactly when Gino died. It's something to talk about because we don't know how to talk about death. What was he wearing, when did it happen—all those things outside."

"Everybody used him—that time he was in the hospital for the tests? Mary had his keys. I saw her! Going through his apartment, taking the booze, looking for money! Pack of jackals. Jackals! Ha!"

Rudi thought Ben was going out the door, but he rotated back.

Rudi said, "People don't do things like that when they're sober."

"Celine knew, Tennessee knew. DeSade—there was a master. All the great ones knew—look at O'Neill! What did they think of human nature? Answer me that? Think you know human nature—fucking jackals. O'Neill—ask him, he'll tell you. Ha, ha!!"

Rudi said, "We have to act as if it's better."

Ben looked at Rudi, scowling. "Shit, shit. I suppose, I suppose. I tell you—you do that, and I'll do what I know is right. Vultures and jackals—they'll tear your heart out. Who wins in this fucking country? Who's elected? Who has the money? People who are goody-goody?

People who think man is a noble creature? Rudi, for God's sake, open your eyes. Hee, hee."

"What good is it to think man is bad? What would that do to me? I'd feel worse."

"Do what you want, do what you want. I don't give a damn, I don't care." Ben's teeth ground together producing a scratching sound from behind his closed lips. "Why should I care?" Ben wrapped his old trench coat around him and punched an army field hat down on his white bristles. The door banged shut.

Rudi faced the empty lobby. He felt a great sadness that extended beyond Gino's death.

Rudi looked used. The wrinkles on the corners of his eyes had multiplied; his mouth pursed. Rudi looked through the window on his right into the cold barren street. He saw Ben on the corner watching people crossing Lexington Avenue.

# Alex

Alexandra Hopkins—tall, pale, lean, long blond hair, sharp sunken blue eyes—watched the guy through the open door to the Odyssey kitchen. He was young, thin and pimply with a hint of tattoo on his rolled-up sleeves. His yellow rubber gloves sunk halfway into the gray soapy water twitched over the bottom of the sink for silverware. He was bent over the sink, absorbed, but his head was somewhere else; every few seconds his head swiveled slowly towards the door as if he were planning an escape.

He'll always be a dishwasher. No education, closed eyes, drunk, callow. If she talked to him, she'd ask him what his goals were, ask him what kind of a chance he had of getting them. She would make him think.

Really? And how well has that worked? Did she help or just annoy? And why? Was it because of Michigan, that faraway unforgettable country with its mashed steel, red edges, and blasted hope? She decided almost daily to change, to let people alone, to mellow—wasn't that the phrase du jour—and then minutes or hours later she went back to helping. If it was hard for her to change, how could she expect it of others?

Alex's tight black sweater and leather jacket made her seem a pale flower nudging out of dark bracts. She turned away from that view across the maze of Odyssey booths and stared through her reflection at the surging crowds. She was waiting for one of the waitresses, Calley Mirona. Calley was tall, a curly brunette, full body, ready smile, and blood-red polished nails worn into half-moons. Calley asked her if she wanted to have a drink after work. Alex, surprised, said yes. Calley was outgoing and friendly, and when they chatted, connected on some pessimistic current. At least that was what Alex thought.

Calley was frisky and talkative as she led her through after-work knots of people on Lexington scurrying home or queued at the doors of bars or restaurants. She led her to her favorite bar/restaurant, Tommy's. Old Tommy's, Calley explained while fluttering her hands at invisible fixtures, was stained oak, cathedral back-bar, sawdust, and determined

Kip's Bay alcoholics. New Tommy's, the extant Tommy's, was black and gray with the pretend elegance of a new high-rise lobby.

At the door, Calley said, "I like it cuz it's close."

Alex surveyed the crowd, remarking the bar top which ran with twin mirrors in front and back of the bar, the mirror in front stopping where the restaurant started, the back-bar mirror running the length of Tommy's. She turned to Calley. "Always the best reason."

Alex followed Calley past the octagonal window, a ragged eye on Lexington's bustle, and settled at the street end of the long black bar top.

Calley said, "Hey, thanks for coming. This is on me."

Alex said, "Thanks. I'll take a vodka tonic."

"I used to drink those, but there's not enough booze. I don't have time. I suppose I should try to moderate at least one of my vices. I'm full of them: cigarettes, booze, kids—there's a vice I could do without."

"What about husbands?" Alex said, amused at Calley's recitation.

"Mother lode! Husbands are diseases; they attach to you when you're young, suck you dry and leave you drinking, smoking, and coping. Know what's funny?"

Alex sat up straight. She listened to Calley, but her attention had already wandered from her long pale hands to the surge of secretaries, bond salesmen, and businessmen from mid-Manhattan crowding the bar, the tinkling glasses, snatches of conversation, lingering odors of smoke and lemon Pledge. She supposed the crowd would split soon, some crowding through the door on their way to a commute or a Kip's Bay condo, others following their second drink into the back where they would eat, listen to mood music, and find their profile in Tommy's mirrors.

Alex half-turned towards Calley. "What's funny?"

"Bob, my jerkaholic husband. He's a Cancer!" Calley beat a tinkly staccato on the bar top and laughed. "A Cancer! You know what I said about husbands and disease. God, it fits so well you want to cry. Hey, Mac! Drinks!"

A bartender's thick neck came up from another conversation. "Calley, haven't I been taking care of you?" He walked towards them, bandy-legged, tiny eyes half-lidded.

"Mac, Alex."

"My pleasure," said Mac, winking at Alex. "We need more young blood in here." He turned back to Calley and put his rough hand over hers. Calley stroked his hand and looked into his eyes.

Calley nervously slipped her hand from under Mac's. "I almost forgot why we're here. Let's start with a vodka tonic and a vodka martini with a whisper of vermouth."

"You got it, beautiful."

A hundred Macs retreated down the bar in dueling reflections in the bar's mirrors.

Alex unbuttoned her coat and edged into a more comfortable perch on the barstool. She was sure Calley wanted her as a buffer in a sex pas de deux. That was all right. It was good getting out of the Rex. Good forgetting. She regarded the single men in Tommy's, ties loosened, coats opened, watches flashing, incipient grins. One-night stand, the game, slap and tickle, vamoose. Was that what Calley meant about having a good time?

Calley said, "Mac's a great guy—got personality, a job he likes, and he's great with the ladies. I'm tempted."

"And your Cancer?" Alex said, bemused.

"He has girlfriends; I know all about it. Doesn't bother me. It's fun listening to his excuses. In a couple years, when the kids are older, Bob is going to wake up in the garbage. Say, did you ever think you were stuck in another era? You know your body and spirit in the 90s, and when you get home, hello 50s! You know, stay together for the kids, don't hurt the kids, blah, blah, blah. I pretend, pretend, pretend. What about you? I've been babbling about my problems. You got a guy; plan on kids? You know the routine."

Alex said, "I tell people I live without elaborate expectations. It might even be true."

A hundred fractured Macs returned with their drinks.

Mac slid the vodka tonic over to Alex and the vodka martini to Calley. He winked at Alex and put his thick hand over Calley's.

Alex knew Mac's type. He knew the scoop before anyone else. Typical. On top of the world. Mac would have distant goals, dreams, fantasies. He might even know they were illusions. He wouldn't care. In ten years, he would still be in Tommy's, still pushing drinks, still putting, or trying to put, his hand over women's hands...but the women would be older, and Mac would be jaded, tired, wondering where the years went. Like,

Alex thought, the older locals now, the psychic distance making them shake their heads slowly at fraying memories.

And Calley. Stuck, stuck as the pimply guy up to his elbows in grease and garbage. But she thought she could escape the cycle, that around the next corner was a guy who would make it right. How did people have that capacity, that resilient capacity to dupe themselves?

Mac said, "On me—damn it's hard to keep good-looking women in this place."

Calley laughed, stroked Mac's hand, then slipped the other one out from underneath. "I have to watch it—I could get used to this."

Mac was called down the bar. He walked down the bar with a rocking gait.

Calley took a long drink of her martini, then tapped her wedding ring against the cocktail glass. She said, "What do you think?"

Alex shrugged. "Another man, another melodrama. It's your life."

Calley gulped her drink. "I know that, but I want to try. Just because you know it won't work never stops you from trying. Mac! Another vodka martini!"

Alex sipped her vodka tonic. Heat. It was a warm pleasant feeling.

Booze was the ultimate shield. How people dreamed when loosened up! What to dream about? Making it in the Big Rotten Apple? That was one of her dreams, once upon a time.

"You look preoccupied," said Calley.

Alex finished her drink and set it down carefully on a coaster. "Revisiting past daydreams. Isn't that what one does in bars?"

"About?"

"Writing, novels, making it big. It seems naïve now."

"We should all have dreams, shouldn't we?"

Alex shrugged. "Depends. I don't live in the past. And I have to go to the bathroom."

"Opening across from the waitress station."

"Right." Alex edged her way through the thinning crowd. A score of mirror Alexes followed her through the reflected heads, elbows, and drinks.

When she came back, Mac was huddled with Calley. When she came up, Mac was called down the bar.

Alex said, "Thanks for the drink, but I think it's time to go."

"So early. Look, the piano player's coming on for an early set."

"Sorry. Don't you have to catch a train?"

"There's always another one. Stay here while I call the kids."

Alex watched Mac. His piggish eyes followed Calley. It looked like Calley, despite what she said about men, was going to try another one.

Calley came back beaming. "Mac, set 'em up. Calley's free for a couple hours."

Alex started towards the door. "Thanks again."

"I'll see you in the Odyssey."

"More than likely."

Mac strutted towards Calley. Calley loosened up on her chair.

Alex glanced back through the open door.

The end of that affair. Calley depressed, Mac unconscious, happy. Seeing it happen after Calley's attitude towards men was almost depressing. It was what she saw about the people she talked to, the Rex tenants. They all said they agreed with her, that their dreams or goals were impossible, then they went back to dreaming, to being deceived, to living lies.

* * *

Alex stared out at a cold gray Saturday. Through the row houses and small apartment buildings, people walked briskly on Twenty-eighth Street, but bulking Park Avenue apartment buildings blocked the view further west. Past Park and the Hudson and New York and the states in between lay her home, that abandoned place.

She closed her eyes. She blocked it out. The bloody images recurred. She supposed her primitive brain forced images on the conscious one. She opened her eyes and fingered the edge of her shirt. She regarded her primly made bed with a critical eye. She hadn't intended to live in the Rex long, a week at the most, but inertia took over. After two weeks she had her room fumigated, the floor waxed and buffed, the walls painted a dull gold, and a new bed put in, a dresser, and a stuffed chair from which she gazed at Midtown. She explained to herself that she was retrenching. After

Michigan, after the last year in Manhattan. She needed time to retrench, to live in the present. Wasn't that what she said in the last hotel?

An image of Michigan yo-yoed back, bloody, violent, crushing.

Alex regarded herself in the alcove mirror. An incipient frown had etched tiny lines around her dark eyes. Blush on pale cheeks, pale pink lipstick. She brushed her blond hair roughly.

She snatched up her black wool coat and struggled putting it on.

She rummaged through the top of her drawer. She stuffed her black gloves and black wallet in her coat.

She locked her room and let out her breath. There were times when that image seared her brain all day, days when she went to movies, or started meaningless conversations in bars.

She hurried towards the elevator. Early morning sounds followed her: radios, TVs, the splash of water in a bathroom, a toilet flushing. The lobby was empty, Ivan dozing, slumped on his hand in the clerk's half-circle. One reason she lived in the Rex was for people. There were always people about, always people to distract her, not her kind of people, but people.

She walked down the worn steps. January chill. Outside, Ben the Hermit stood on the corner staring at a green light. She watched him wait until it was red, then cross. Why was he still alive? Did he live a life without illusion? Ben's head dipped into his army coat and pushed out. Her life would not be like Ben's. You didn't have to be a shabby hermit to live without illusions.

People hurried by, bundled, cold, preoccupied. A BMW sped towards the light on Lexington as if it were racing the Devil. Alex walked slowly towards Park. She thought of going to the Odyssey but instead turned and walked slowly downtown, images of Michigan flickering in her mind. Those images formed a red wall around her. Would they follow her forever? Too early for a drink. Who was that? Bel Benaventura. Which floor was she on? Five? She was an editor and had a daughter who lived at the Rex once. Alex hurried and joined Bel.

"Mind if I walk along?"

Bel looked at her and gave her wry smile. "Not at all."

They walked in step under a lightening sky down Park Avenue to Union Square. They chatted occasionally about the weather, the traffic, but most of the time they walked silently. Bel wanted breakfast and Alex went along.

Bel turned into the Star Deli off Union Square. They sat at a counter where they saw people walking on the street and in the square.

Bel had lox, bagels and cream cheese, Alex black coffee.

"So different in the fall," said Bel, nodding towards the barren square. "About now, the vans and trucks would arrive with fresh flowers and apples, squash, pumpkins, and fall produce stacked in wooden crates. It is a fading season, but bountiful. Now it's blasted. Persephone in Hades."

"It's clean," said Alex.

Bel took a bite of her bagel. She said, muffled, "Empty."

"I suppose it's a matter of perspective," said Alex, stirring her coffee absently, fingers gripped loosely on the long spoon. "A glass half full or empty."

Bel set her bagel down and looked at Alex directly. "What are you doing at the Rex?"

Alex's mouth was a black thread across her face. Alex's hands closed around the mug warming her hands. "Regrouping. Isn't that what most people are doing?"

"I assumed that. I don't mean to be nosey, but several people have told me they don't like you. You're young, good looking, bright. Why would they say that?"

"I don't know." Alex glanced quickly at Bel, then the knot of people at the counter. She spoke into the air. "I talk to them, listen to them. I suppose I'm struck by their aspirations. They seem outlandish, out of reach. If they're regrouping, they should be realistic, or try to be."

"But what do you say?"

Alex stared into her mug. Overhead lights flashed in the black coffee. "I talk to them about how I live, or try to live, in the present without illusions. I don't insult anyone; I just tell them what I do. At times I think I'm helping them. Wouldn't they be happier if they lived without illusions?"

Bel thought for a few seconds, her dark brows tightening slightly. "You criticize their dreams. I might find that interesting; at least it's different. Perhaps you're a crusader."

Alex laughed. "I don't believe in white bearded men in the sky."

Bel shrugged. "Quest?"

Alex frowned. "Appropriate if I were looking for anything."

"Maybe that's your problem."

Alex laughed and shook her head slowly as if she had been completely misunderstood. "Psychobabble. To live in the present without illusions is a problem? Flesh that out for me. Shouldn't everyone strive for that and not some typically unreachable goal?"

"I'm editing a book called *The Shallows*. It's about superficiality. I agree people should try to live in the present and shouldn't give in to our superficial culture. But people have goals too, dreams; it's part of being human."

Alex shrugged. "When it comes to it, they don't have to talk to me."

Bel said, "You're an anomaly. People want to know who you are. That's why they talk to you, and it's human nature to talk about aspirations. They should know better by now."

Alex shrugged. "They do. Most tenants avoid me. What about you?"

Bel grimaced. "You want to dig into Bel Benaventura, my illusions? It's poor stuff."

Alex laughed. "You make me sound like a detective. I don't dig."

Bel said, "Do you think people give up their goals, their dreams, because of you?"

The café was filling up. A couple in parkas opened the door and hurried inside. The edge of Alex's napkin lifted slightly in the draft, then fell back. The couple stamped their feet dramatically and trooped to an open booth. Alex pulled the top of her coat over her throat. "Most people ignore me, I suppose, and go back dreaming."

"I can't believe you're goalless, or dreamless."

Alex wrapped her coat tightly around herself. Her dark eyes took on a fleeting look. "Once."

"What?"

Alex felt her lips tighten. "It doesn't matter. I left it back in Michigan. Writing. It's history."

Bel shrugged, "Maybe I can help. I know agents, publishers."

"Not anymore." Alex drew herself up, eased off her stool, and started towards the door. She stopped, turned. "Most people don't give up their illusions; I did."

Bel said, "Did you decide to give them up, or have to?"

Alex shook her head, turned and pushed the door open.

People huddled by hurrying from warm place to warm place. The weather constrained life, upstaging the journey with resting points. Alex walked towards the Village. Talking to Bel was a mistake. She wanted to blank out, but Bel brought it right back. Alex walked slowly down Broadway thinking about what Bel said, fractured images of Michigan poking at her consciousness. The pale sun played hide-and-seek with thin clouds and occasionally painted the windows on Broadway a weak gold.

\* \* \*

"Hi, Kurt." Kurt turned from talking to Ivan.

Kurt was a philosophy student at Columbia. Kurt was impatient with academia, his professors. A few days ago, Alex had listened patiently to his reasons for rejecting school. At one point, she thought he was a fellow traveler, someone who had given up illusions. But then he started talking about forming his own perfect philosophy starting from scratch sans preconceptions. Kurt likened himself to Kant and Hegel.

Kurt, all philosophies are false, have to be. How will yours be any different? How can you create anything new? And how can you create anything new here in the Rex? Aren't you fooling yourself? Aren't you making the same mistake every philosopher has made thinking that theirs is the one true philosophy and others wrong? Why can't you live freely in the present?

Kurt hurried past her out the door, his tangle of dark curls bobbing once in the small square door window and disappearing.

Alex stood in the middle of the lobby between the closing door and the elevator. Why did people take themselves so seriously? Alex opened the elevator gate, got in, and punched her floor.

When she opened the gate on her floor, she was in a thoughtful mood, thinking of Kurt and why one would try to philosophize, why one would bank their life, their existence on it. It was an esoteric way of keeping life at a distance. She walked around the elevator housing. Margaret was opening her door as she passed.

"Hi, Margaret."

A frown filled Margaret's creased face, and she hurriedly shut the door.

Alex moved close to Margaret's door. "Margaret, I just want to talk."

"Ggggg o aaaaway."

Alex's cheek tugged down in a frown as she walked slowly to her door.

Margaret wanted to be singer and intended to take voice lessons. They sat in the lobby for a few minutes while Margaret told her how she was going to do it, how she was going to save her money, get a coach, find an agent, and start as an act in a small café.

How reasonable is it to get lessons at your age? Don't you have to work on the stutter first? Work as an office temp isn't so bad. Wouldn't you feel better if you admitted that to yourself? Wouldn't you feel as if a load has been lifted from your back?

Margaret was obviously offended. But in five years or ten, Margaret would still be temping, and she'd feel worse, her dreams contained in the smudged address of a coach, a handful of formal rejection letters, a well-thumbed copy of *Talent Search*.

Alex decided to see Eric. At least he'd talk to her. Eric's door was cracked open, and she saw he was crawling on the floor. He raised his hand and brought it down hard. She pushed the door wide with her gloved forefinger.

He glanced at her, frowned, and pushed a wad of toilet paper towards her. "Roach."

Eric was tall, thin, and had floppy blond hair that fell over the top of his glasses. Eric had a long neck, even collar bones, white skin, freckles. His open closet door showed stacks of sweaters, shirts on plastic hangers, and a shoe tree full of polished shoes. Crumpled papers littered the floor near the table and the typewriter. Over the brass bed, the Piranesi print added a spider web of complication to the room.

Alex rested her arm against the door. Beyond her hazy reflection in Eric's window, the Olympia bisected the skyline. "How's the play?"

Eric picked at a loose thread on his sweater, frowned, and looked away. "All right."

"A random mix of moguls, property, and blond-haired playwrights, hubris, and the fall."

"Why do you make everything sound so unreal?" Eric paused. "It's true, right now, I need more material. I've got the outline, the map, but I need more filler."

"Doesn't it sound a little like paint by numbers with words?"

Eric frowned. "I don't want to talk about it with you."

He would strive, pen a few words every day, and cross them out at night, like Penelope's web woven during the day and unwoven at night. And drugs. The drugs will offer him the illusion of success. He would use more until he wouldn't know if he were writing or not, or if it mattered. People think they're impregnable, shored up behind the fortress of the personality.

Eric walked to the desk, realized what he was carrying, squeezed the wad of paper in his hand, and threw it into a small shiny black wastebasket. Then he disappeared into the alcove where Alex heard the sound of running water. When he came out, he stared at her.

Alex, abashed, turned and walked slowly towards the elevator.

* * *

The Rex was a storehouse of dreamers. Did they know their dreams were dust? Sometimes she thought she should nod and agree with everyone. Wouldn't that be a lie? But when she met someone new, she told them what she thought. Isn't that what self-help gurus, therapists of any sort, born-agains, AA do? They destroy the person in order to create a sanitized one with a new diet, a new drug, a new god. Weren't the replacements just as bad, just as illusory, as the original dreams?

She'd talked to many Rex residents. But she wasn't naïve; they would revert to type, they would continue dreaming. Perhaps she instilled a shard of doubt in their minds. Perhaps it would make them pause and think about who they really were. Because, she explained to herself, isn't that what one *should* want in life? Wasn't Polonius' dictum of being true to oneself true? Wasn't that what everyone should strive for and not shroud one's true nature in illusions?

It was time to leave the Rex. It happened in the last place. She was shunned, frowned upon, ridiculed in secret. She was human. She didn't want to be a leper. It was odd; she needed to be around people, needed the connection, but when she talked to them...

The Monday after she and Calley had their drink in Tommy's, she was walking back from checking out The Shades, a better West Side hotel, when she saw the guy on the stoop a few doors down from the Rex. She'd seen him before, but he was part of the background of Twenty-eighth Street, of a particular renovated town house with white trim and green shutters. He sat on the cement stoop with its antique wrought-iron seraphim, cinched up in a worn tan London Fog coat, sipping out of a paper bag held with long glabrous fingers. He was hatless (in this weather?), wore khaki pants, scuffed brown shoes, and white socks which clumped on the top of his shoes revealing thin blue-veined legs. He was tall with loose straight hair, lanky, a long seamed face, grizzled chin. He should have been cold in that weather, but he sat there, a gaunt gargoyle balancing the wrought cupids, all rag and bone.

She walked past him, his thin mumbling a receding Doppler. On the worn Rex steps she turned. Vagabond thoughts peppered her consciousness: Who was he? Why was he sitting there? What was in the sack? What was he saying? Beyond obvious questions, his isolation bothered her. He seemed to have a special isolation in a city that specialized in isolation and loneliness. He seemed to have isolated his entire being, body, soul, and spirit.

She found out the next day from a few random encounters his name was Bert, although no one knew exactly why he did what he did. Some deep hurt, they thought. A hurt that made him that way. He lived on eight in front and was on SSI.

The next few days she organized her time so she could watch Bert. Was he a mental defective, subnormal? She didn't think so. She began to think that in his simplicity, he lived without illusions. Yes, that was it. He was a kind of spiritual ideal, except for one thing: he wasn't quite human. He didn't talk to anyone. Would she become like that, her spirit bound with tighter and tighter stitches until she whispered to imaginary people?


Alex walked down the worn Rex steps and turned toward Park Avenue. She was on her way to the Village, to a new bar, the Grotto on Seventh Avenue. She'd found a fleeting companionship in the last few days in that bar. They greeted her; several patrons talked to her. And they seemed without illusions, possibly cynical. If she lived in The Shades, she could take a West Side bus and be in the Grotto in a few minutes.

She stared at Bert. He had begun to stand out against the jagged-topped row houses spreading unevenly towards Park Avenue. His pale fingers held his sack loosely. She approached him and stared at him from a few feet away. He gestured with his sack, as if to an invisible interlocutor. Then he hesitated, stopped, shook his head as if agreeing to what had been said. He talked right through her.

Bert dipped his head contritely and said softly, "No, no. It's not that easy."

Maybe she was attracted to him because of body type. They were both tall, lean, although Bert was bonier. His angular hard face with its deep etchings matched in a way her own. While she stared at him, she got the same eerie sensation of seeing herself in some corner, drink in hand, spirit bound tight, babbling to herself.

She had to try to talk to him. She had plenty of time later to dope out her motives. She thought she wanted to prove that anyone that isolated could be brought back. If he could be brought back, she could. There was a middle ground in the present; there had to be.

"Hey."

Bert's milky blue eyes stared past her. Words emerged through his frosty breath. "Yes, that's right, too right. But what can you do? What does it matter?"

Alex stepped closer and looked straight into Bert's unseeing eyes. "Talk to me."

Bert raised the brown paper sack to this mouth and sipped. "No, no. That can't be right. That's never right."

"Bert!"

"There is no point?"

She leaned forward a foot from Bet. "That's just it, Bert. What is the point?"

His sack brushed her chin. He drank.

Alex drew herself up. Her eyes were flinty, her face taut. Bert was beyond her ideal, over the edge. They'd both suffered, both given up their hopes. But he'd gone too far. She had to bring him back. Perhaps the only thing stopping him from coming back was alcohol.

"Bert, listen to me!"

Bert stared past her, as he had the first time, but he stopped talking.

They stayed like that for a few long seconds; then she said, "Talk to me."

Bert stared at her. His eyes were milky, clouded. His hand clutched his brown paper sack, closer to his body.

She said, "You don't need that beer. Talk to me. Come back." Alex grabbed at Bert's sack but Bert snatched it away from her. He brought the sack to his lips and slurped. He said past her, "No, no. That can't be right. You're always saying that, and nobody listens." Bert paused, then said, "But maybe you are right. I can't be right all the time, can I?"

Alex screamed at Bert, "Quit hiding behind your stupid malt liquor!" Brucie stared at her from the steps of the Rex.

Alex wrapped herself tightly in her coat and hurried towards Park.


Bert became an obsession. She wasn't sure when the idea came to her. Later, her plan seemed the product of her own increasing isolation, or misperception. The plan she thought up in her walks through the city, her dinners at the Odyssey, her drinks in the Grotto, was to get that malt liquor away from him. With that prop gone, Bert would have to talk to her. He would reveal what his hurt was; he would live a normal life free of illusion.

Outside it was bleak, overcast. She stared at the phone.

She snatched up the phone and called the police. She explained that Bert was annoying the pedestrians and that he needed either a social worker or psychological help.

The next day, Bert was gone.

She asked Rudi about him.

Rudi frowned. "He wasn't hurting anybody. I tried to explain that, but the police said that they would get him help."

Alex said, "How do you know? People don't sit on stoops and talk to imaginary people. Maybe he could live without a prop; maybe he could lead a normal life without illusions."

"Maybe he didn't need help."

"Some people need more help than others."

The next few days, Bert's spot was empty. It almost seemed as if part of the street were missing. Finally, she asked Rudi about Bert again. Rudi stared at the yellowed pages of his ledger.

She said, "Is he in rehab?"

Rudi shook his head. "No, no."

Alex frowned. "Well he should be. What's taking them so long?"

Rudi shook his head and idly thumbed his ledger. "They put him in detox...they say he quit talking altogether. Yesterday, he tried to hang himself with his belt. He's in the hospital; they don't know if he'll make it."

Alex trembled. Her whole body shook. "That didn't happen!"

Rudi stared at her. "It did."

She staggered towards the elevator. "If I only knew, but who can know?"

Rudi yelled after her. "If we only knew what?"

Alex said, "Nothing, nothing."

* * *

Alex let the sun draw her away from a feeling of emptiness. She'd stayed in her room for a day, except for two furtive forays for take-out. She didn't want to see anyone, especially Rex tenants. She closed her eyes and tried to forget. The sun slanted through the worn frame and made skewed rectangles on the waxed floor. She felt an eddy of cold air around her neck. She tried to forget, to make her mind blank, but Bert was always there, a fey thin figure. Her imagination took her to a bare cell, a chair, Bert carefully undoing his belt, tying it to a pipe, kicking the chair away. He would swing there, a sock slipping off his foot revealing his thin bare leg. She finally realized that his malt liquor protected him from the abyss. She'd taken his prop away. Did we all need props? Was there a hidden part of all of us, either a dream or a barrier that keeps the darkness out?

She got up and walked restlessly to the door and back to the window. Every few minutes, unbidden, bloody images of Michigan, of metal and flesh and fire, of lost hopes and dreams flooded her brain.

"I have to leave here."

She knew she had to leave the Rex, and she had to leave Kip's Bay.

That West Side hotel? She had a recurring image of herself at some distant time. It was the fleeting image that pierced the blood images of Michigan and Bert in his cell. Bert. She was aged, bored, a drink in her hand in a bar like Tommy's nervously tapping a cigarette into a blackened ashtray. She was a husk, the only thing left pills or the trigger.

*Rap, rap.*

Alex stopped halfway to the window. She hesitantly went to the door.

"Who is it?"

"I'm Frieda Berg. I live on eight."

Alex, frowning, opened the door.

She was wary of Frieda, but she wasn't sure why. There was something indestructible about her, or dangerous. "What's this about?" Alex said nervously and more rudely than she'd intended.

"You leaving the Rex."

Alex let out a sharp laugh. She had to leave, but no one could force her to go. "Why would I want to leave? I can stay where I want."

Frieda smiled malevolently. "You've managed to depress, insult, and in one case destroy a Rex tenant. That's unacceptable."

Alex sighed, slumped. "I was speaking my mind, trying to be truthful, trying to be helpful. People don't want to hear it. And I know I have to leave. Oh Christ. I didn't know, I didn't know." She looked at Frieda, hesitantly, then defiantly. "You can't force me to go."

"Research," said Frieda.

Alex frowned. "What?"

"I'm good at it. I often wonder why I'm in IM Investigations at all. But I'm good at it. Finding things out: research, putting things together, making connections."

Alex tightened her fingers on the edge of the door. Her eyes rotated away from Frieda, and she stared at a stain on the carpet.

"What kind of research?"

Frieda said, "I think you've guessed. I know about Michigan. I know you're rich, and I know you've lived in other hotels."

Alex seemed to shrink, as if she'd aged. "Oh."

"Oddly, I feel for you. I don't know what I would have done. Something terrible, I suppose. Something self-lacerating. And I've had shocks. All my family, the family I loved, are gone. And I have a lousy love life and a lousy job. I don't want to make this a melodrama."

"I suppose it is too late."

"You've caused too much damage. If you stay here, I'll make sure everyone knows. The Rex grapevine is fast and occasionally gets it right. It will get it right this time." Frieda hesitated, then said, "Even though you didn't ask, it might relieve you to know Bert will be okay."

* * *

Alex took a room in The Shades. She had a last dinner at the Odyssey. Calley waited on her and insisted on a last drink at Tommy's.

She went along, but she hadn't felt the same since Bert's suicide attempt and Frieda's threat. She felt nervous, more alone than at the last hotel. The vision of a gaunt dreamless Alex in a West Side bar haunted her.

It was the middle of the week, and Tommy's was half full. The gladiolus at the end of the bar were withered, brown, and swayed when the Tommy's door opened.

Calley said, "Vodka tonic?"

"What you're drinking. I want to get there faster too."

"Denny, two vodka martinis!" Calley turned to Alex. "I almost didn't want to come here."

"Why not?"

Calley shrugged. "Mac, Mr. Love-em and Leave-em. It was okay, but you always think there will be more. Like I said, we're built that way. Anyway, I knew Denny was on tonight."

A few minutes later, Calley tapped her glass. "Here's to a good life."

"Sure."

"You don't seem too happy. Guy problem?"

"No, thinking about the future."

"I knew you wouldn't last in that hotel."

"There's always another one." Alex gulped her drink. She should have felt the heat but didn't feel a thing.

# Rocky

Rocky Morceau scratched the tattoo coiled around his arm. Armband from a distance, close it clarified into a rattlesnake with rattles in gray and yellow, body winding around his bicep in yellow, brown, and sharp gray diamonds. The head, stopping inches from the top of his shoulder, had flinty red eyes, ebony fangs, and a blood-red, deep mouth. Rocky liked the tattoo and sometimes admired it in whatever mirror was handy— the mirror over the sink, or the small bubbled mirror in the common bathroom at the Rex, or in Mariam's art nouveau one. Occasionally he thought about what tattoos mean. He thought of marines, ex-cons, tough guys, and usually, finally, backward cultures in Africa, Borneo, or New Zealand, where tattoos represented the mythos of their tribe or the spirit of a crow. Despite esoteric reasons, tattoos, thanks to Madison Avenue, MTV, and adenoidal rock stars, had become the rage.

But no. He got his on an impulse to make him someone different, to lead him in a different direction. He got it a few months after he left Boise. He felt down, as low as when Claire, his mother, died, and later his father, Doc. The tattoo lifted his spirits but didn't quite give him a new persona.

"Who cares about rationale?" Mariam said, tracing the snake head with her index finger. She tucked her slim legs underneath herself and backed up to a middle distance in the corner of the bed. Sounds from Greenwich Village seeped through the closed barred window off her shoulder. She poised her index finger under her chin and considered. "It's violent but somehow acts as a counterpoint to how you appear, to your softness."

"That was kind," said Rocky, grinning. "You mean this wreck of a face?"

Mariam was small with a classic straight nose, auburn curls, and soft brown eyes. She owned and ran Avedya, a small shop specializing in vintage clothes on Bleeker Street. She was a fixture in the neighborhood and every Thursday went to Oracle, a local Village bar. She met Rocky there six months ago. Rocky had gotten used to her tics, the way she poised her finger under her chin, the occasional sidelong wink of complicity.

"Neither of us are movie stars," Mariam said, smiling warmly, then winking. "But we're interesting looking. Know what I mean?"

Rocky laughed. "You're a cameo, I'm a mug shot, but I like that."

Mariam drew closer to Rocky, smiled, traced her finger over the covers near his shoulder. "Me too. Let me see that tattoo again."

Rocky: Army brat, college dropout, ex-bar owner, ex-roughneck, ex-Golden Gloves boxer with one bent ear and a slightly mangled face. He was a few pounds overweight, had a tangle of curly graying black hair, and heavy, puffy hands. Young Rocky was quick to anger, brash, but time had created a slight, lopsided smile Mariam said made him look vaguely handsome, an Albert Finney look-alike.

Rocky knew it was about time to leave, to go back to the Rex. But lately he'd delayed leaving. He liked Mariam, and he liked her apartment and the Village. Somehow he knew if he stayed more, it would change everything.

\* \* \*

Monday, back at the Rex, Rocky called Morris. No, Morris said, both Staley and I are working and we don't need you today. Rocky shook his head at the phone and thought, as he'd thought before, it was about time to look for another bartending job. The No Exit was a steady gig when Staley was sick, but he'd been okay that winter.

Down, aimless, Rocky bundled up and scuffed through the city, warmed infrequently by memories of the weekend. He hunkered over a weak coffee in a Chock full o'Nuts near the Empire State Building and spent an hour reading the *Times* in the New York Public Library. Finally he settled into a worn seat left of center in the Markee, a rattrap Times Square movie theatre.

The Markee was a thousand-seat theatre filled with the memories of openings, limos, actors, silk gowns, and glittering jewels. It had decayed for decades, the green-gilt interior fading, the gold paint peeling, seats broken, rugs tattered, refreshment stand shuttered. Rocky didn't care; it felt right, secure.

He saw two films that day—he couldn't remember which—and, resigned, was halfway out of his seat when another movie bloomed on the screen. His intermission—odd, he remembered, how movies sometimes were more than an intermission, were in some ways more real than life—was over. In the last few minutes of whatever film he was watching, he'd given into a vague Rocky Morceau depression. He had a Mariam-less evening ahead of him, the only prospect meatloaf at Plato's, listening to the creaking sounds of an old hotel, and twisting the bent antenna of his tiny TV hoping for a channel.

He edged back down in his worn seat left/center of the screen.

*Snapshot* was silent with few subtitles. The first and one of the only subtitles announced the name of the main character. Willie was *Snapshot*. Willie was moon-faced with almond-shaped Mongolian eyes. He was not tall but had a knot of a body, wiry like an oak. It was easy to see that people would make the mistake of thinking Willie simple, except beneath a placid expression, his brown eyes glowed with intelligence. Rocky's first impression, one which lasted through several *Snapshot* trailers, was one of innocence. Willie was ready for the world, ready to inhale life, ready to seize life with his strong hands, but he knew nothing. His character was Locke's tabula rasa, a celluloid *Candide*.

Rocky felt a kinship with Willie. He supposed it was because the director was trying to create an Everyman, a universal type posing his boot tentatively on the shifting sands and quicksand-patch path of life.

When *Snapshot* ended abruptly, it surprised Rocky. The Markee didn't show trailers, but that's what it seemed it was. He thought about checking with the projectionist but decided not to. He was hungry and it was time for that meatloaf.

The next day he had his usual check-in with Morris at eleven. No sub, no job. He bought a copy of the *Times* and read the want ads over lunch at the Odyssey. Afterwards, outside, Rocky sifted his options for the day. The cold snap had eased. A walk in Central Park? Long walk to the Battery? No. Rocky, jobless, gravitated towards Times Square and the Markee. Growing up in Germany or Korea or Fort Dix, the major connection with his slight mother, Claire, and burly father, Mick "Doc" Morceau, was the base theatre. After Claire died, movies became more important. He and Doc saw everything. It was a way of connecting obliquely, the screen a surrogate Claire.

Rocky paid two bucks to the half-idiot Leon and strolled slowly into the Markee. He settled into his favorite seat and watched two Fred Astaire/Ginger Rogers musicals. They lifted him out of a vague depression. What a period! The Great Depression, starvation, unemployment, dust bowls. Fred and Ginger waltzed obliviously through lavish sets with rapturous smiles on their faces. He was in their fantasy world and felt the letdown when they rolled the credits.

Rocky felt for his money, his gloves, rubbed his eyes, dragged his thick hand through his graying curls, and stood up. He was walking up the aisle buttoning his jacket when the thin introductory music of *Snapshot* made him turn. He sat down in the nearest seat, anticipating the same trailer. It was a different one. That trailer showed Willie in a drab unidentified European city full of soot and skewed Gothic buildings. The setting reminded him of German films like *Caligari* and *Faust*, expressionist, silent, and full of shadows. Willie had an apartment and a delivery job. A girlfriend! Willie's face radiated calmness. Willie was happy. Odd, Rocky thought, he'd only seen two trailers and he wanted Willie to stay like that. But we all have to move, to change. It was a law of emotional physics. Rocky wondered vaguely what the film would be like...obstacles, loss, redemption?

When the trailer ended, Rocky's curiosity was peaked. The Markee didn't show trailers, especially trailers of silent Eastern European films. Rocky knew the Markee projectionist Hal Moody. Rocky, puzzled, unhooked the rope to the balcony and walked up the long curved staircase to the mezzanine and up the short steps to the projection booth.

Hal looked like a vulture. He was bent and bald with sunken dishwater eyes. His long vampirish arms extended past the rolled-up sleeves of a loose white shirt. Hal croaked out a laugh and scraped his scalp with yellow fingernails. "They never finished it."

Rocky squinted into the gloom. "How so?"

"The director—he plays Willie—put a bullet in his head before he finished it."

Rocky felt chill. "What's with the trailers?"

"Filler. Media Mass, the distributor, sends a clip now and then." Hal coughed, a long throaty cough, then said, "There's a cult."

"You're kidding."

"I know this projectionist in Brooklyn. People come just for the trailers. This is New York. You can have a cult about eggshell cartons or lamp sockets."

Rocky frowned. A cult. He could see it. A crazy director, a film never finished where he played the lead. "Weird."

"What's weirder is that I've never been able to figure this guy Willie or what the flick's about. Maybe that's why the guy put a bullet in his head. He couldn't figure it out either."

"Willie seems okay."

"That will change."

* * *

The voice mumbled, unsure.

"Hal. The Markee."

Rocky shifted the phone to his left hand and glanced at the clock. He'd slept late. "Hal, sure. How are you?"

Rocky sat up in bed. He rubbed his eyes with a meaty fist, and his room clarified: books, yesterday's *Times* scattered over the table, a cluster of photos on the dresser. Out the window, through the half-closed shade, the Olympia arched up like an obelisk.

"You said to call," said the raspy voice.

"I did?" said Rocky, thinking back to the last time he'd seen Hal.

"You know," said Hal. "When those trailers came back."

Rocky frowned. *Snapshot*, Willie, his life, the director. "Right."

"I guess you forgot. You told me to call."

He thought about what Hal said. Why would he want to see them? "Are they on?"

"After a couple of noirs...can't say I like them noirs. God, they're bleak."

"For sure. Thanks for calling. Might be over."

"My pleasure."

Rocky cradled the phone.

Should he, shouldn't he? He didn't have anything else, and he liked noirs. Rocky washed up, dressed, and threw on his pea coat. He grabbed his black gloves and wrapped his scarf loosely around his neck.

He walked past the bathroom, through the fire doors, and caught the elevator. He nodded at Rudi at the desk, descended the front steps, and walked quickly to the corner. He glanced at the Olympia and the Giltmore across Lexington Avenue, carefully tucked his scarf into his coat, and hunched against the cold. He crossed the street and walked quickly up Lexington.

He should have taken Park. On Thirty-seventh Street, he stopped across from the OTB. It was a small place with a huge plate-glass window. Bettors stared at the board and crumpled tickets. He felt a physical pull. Marley said he was chasing the American Dream. No, he wanted money for distance, as a barrier between Rocky Morceau and everyone else. At least that's what he told Marley; now he wasn't sure. A year ago, he stared at the board and crumpled his own tickets.

Rocky hunched his shoulders and hurried on. Twenty minutes later, he stood in front of the Markee. It jutted out of a neon ridge of Times Square Triple X peep shows and decayed movie houses. The Markee was the same old shabby palace, the street scummy as ever, strewn with waste, a human sewer. Prime location, prime sleaze. Someday they'd change it.

He cut off his gaze and turned into the Markee. He paid his two bucks to Leon and minutes later settled into his seat. Ten bums slept in the back rows of the theatre, heads hanging, limbs spread. There was a scattering of people on the right, a bald guy asleep five rows in front, head lolling, light from the movie flickering on the right side of his face.

The movies that day were three noir flicks. *Criss Cross* was OK, even though he could never see Burt Lancaster as a wimp. But *Kiss Me Deadly*, vintage Spillane with its day-glow uranium suitcase, was fun. *Out of the Past* depressed him.

After the last frame, Rocky waited. The air in the Markee seemed to heighten.

The first part of the silent *Snapshot* trailer recalled scenes of Willie's start, his girlfriend. She was pleasant but retiring with big dark eyes, naïve as Willie. He wondered how Willie was going to change. His life was idyllic, a dream, almost dull. Rocky picked his way through scenes of his own past, of Claire and Doc, of a score of Army bases. Was he like Willie once? He couldn't remember. He supposed the drek he carried with him masked easy dreaming times.

He felt a slight shift. A man emerged slowly from the shadows, thin, arch, mean-eyed, watching. Who was he? Willie's boss? The trailer blinked off the screen. The screen glowed dully in the darkened theatre. The arching space was quiet, funereal. A bum in rags slowly got to his feet, scratched his head, and shuffled towards the exit.

Why was the man watching Willie? A new movie—he thought it was *Scarlet Street*—spread its cobalt glow over the backs of the seats. That trailer left him with a worm of doubt. Would that evil pasty-face fate lead to Willie's fall? Did he detect a trace of sorrow in Willie's triangular face, a hint of pouches under his almond eyes?

* * *

The next day, jobless, drifting, Rocky went to another theatre and sat through a Marlon Brando revival. Here was Brando in *Apocalypse Now* as Kurtz; here was Brando, a much younger slimmer, sexy Brando, in *Last Tango in Paris*. Both movies were full of tension and violence.

Back at the Rex, he found a message from Morris. Could he sub for him that weekend and next week? He changed and hurried down to the No Exit.

That weekend and the first few days of the next week were his best that winter. He missed seeing Mariam, but it felt good talking to people, especially talking to someone besides Mariam. He settled into the bar rhythm, the small talk, and stepped through the Rex with a spring in his step.

One morning up late, he visited the roof. He'd only been up there once before, even though he lived close to it. Up there he was surrounded by buildings down towards Twenty-third Street, the Olympia and Giltmore across Lex, the huge looming office buildings on Park. It gave him a different perspective. He liked it, but then closer, the roof was barren, the plants dead, the small trees barren of leaves. A few leaves skittered across the roof or banked against the flats. It made him think of the Rex tenants they'd lost that year, Ric and Gino. He didn't know them well, but they were like the dead leaves blowing across the roof.

But babies took their place. It was the season; after the dead of winter, the spring cycled up new life.

Rocky was starting to feel good about living in Manhattan and working when Morris called and said he was better. He saw Mariam that night. They made love. He hadn't seen her for days, but he could tell they were becoming closer. That weekend they went to bars, listened to jazz, and—bundled up, making cones of their breath—sat on a Washington Square bench and watched people. Rocky realized he lived two extremely different lives. There was his life in the Rex, Times Square movie houses, the No Exit. And there was life, a very different life with Mariam. The one started seeming more like a dead end, winter; the other more about life, spring.

When he got back to the Rex, he had a note from Hal Moody about a couple teen slasher movies and another *Snapshot* trailer.

He flipped the note aimlessly with his fingers. *Snapshot*, Willie. He wanted to leave Willie happy, content with his job, his woman. The last trailer hinted something bad would happen. On the other hand, what was the harm in seeing Willie one more time? But teen slashers? Please.

He bundled up. Outside, he walked slowly towards Park and Times Square. Before he had time to think, he was in his usual seat. That day he got a duo of teen slasher flicks. He watched bored as Blacks, Hispanics, Asians, and any minority got knifed, blown up, and decapitated. Bullies, wise-asses, dweebs, and dorks got slashed. Bad girls slashed. Susie Sunshine and Ken Nice Guy—just say no!—emerged bloodied but their spic-and-span lives intact. You couldn't fault Hollywood for ignoring family values.

*Halloween* credits rolled up the screen. There was a pause after the last credit. The pause lengthened. The Markee was silent.

*Snapshot* smashed into the screen.

Rocky, shocked, squirmed. The first few seconds showed a mini-collage of Willie, his girlfriend, the man lurking in the shadows. Then the music became deep, discordant. Willie was in a subterranean jail, the walls thick, the cell dirty. What happened? Where were the accusations, the police, the defense? The darkness and shadows depressed Rocky, but not more than Willie's face. It was worn, lined, sallow. His eyes were dark holes, the only intimation of intelligence, a realization that it was hopeless. The darkness slowly faded on a black limo racing towards the horizon.

Rocky, puzzled, shook his head as he got to his feet. He could see what was happening. It was about the rise and fall of Willie. He got that. But there was something else that nagged at him. He didn't know quite what it was, and he wasn't sure he liked it.

* * *

Rocky decided not see *Snapshot* trailers. He wanted Willie to remain pure, ignorant of any dark side. Then he knew: he felt his own life—his starts and stops, his hesitations and his failures—was playing out on the screen. Perhaps, he thought, the worst ending would be that it never ended, that Willie vacillated between the poles of happiness and despair, dream and nightmare, like a yo-yo. Realistically that might happen. Did the director leave Willie in limbo?

Rocky walked those next days. The bitter cold didn't bother him. He hunched down, drew his jacket tight against his body, and walked. Up the East Side, down the West. He walked to the Battery, and he walked through and around Central Park.

He was unsettled. Work at the No Exit was spotty. He needed something else, something regular. And he needed more money. He stood in front of an OTB on the West Side. Rocky jammed his gloved hands in his pocket and turned away. Back in his room at the Rex, he contemplated the Olympia. He closed his eyes, trying not to think.

*Brrring, brrring.*

Rocky snatched up the phone hoping it was Morris or Mariam. It was Hal. There was another trailer. Rocky thanked him and lay down on the bed. He closed his eyes but couldn't sleep. Finally he got up, pulled on his coat, and headed towards the Markee.

The other movie—he didn't remember what it was—was just ending when he sat down.

*Snapshot* crashed onto the screen.

Rocky gripped the top of the seat in front of him.

Early Willie, happy Willie, innocent Willie, Willie in love, the dungeon, the black limo. Then Willie walked the dark streets of that town, despondent. For the first time, Rocky felt more than a kinship. He *was* Willie. It was how he felt, how he walked the streets, how he felt a twinge of hopelessness which he hid under wavering bravado.

The black limo pulled up behind Willie. Willie stopped. A door opened. Willie looked past the limo, almost as if he were looking at his past, at an innocent time.

Willie drove. The limo crawled slowly through a garbage-littered area of town. Two men got out of the limo and hustled towards a man on the street. They beat him, kicked him. Nail-studded bats rose and fell punching into the man's head until he was bloody, dead.

Rocky shivered. Large drops formed on his forehead.

The limo drove deeper into a dark maze. Willie's face was a smear on the limo's window. At every turn, Willie watched a collage of crimes and criminals. You could see the progression of emotions on his face, the thickening of his face, the narrowing of his eyes. Slowly, Willie's face became rigid, a mask, his eyes twin points of fading light.

The black limo barreled down a dark tunnel with a flickering of red light at the tunnel mouth. The limo was driving Willie straight to hell.

The light didn't come on nor a new movie. Rocky, shaken, got up slowly. He tried to adjust to the darkness, the only light the thin red light from the projection booth. It was almost as if he were there with Willie blanketed by darkness. He touched the backs of seats and felt his way up the aisle. In the lobby, in the half-light from Forty-second Street, he regarded the winding staircase. He unhooked the rope to the balcony and, hand on rail, walked up the tattered staircase carpet.

Hal appeared seconds after he knocked, looking as ghostly and unkempt as Rocky remembered. They shook hands. Hal said, "Thought I saw you down there."

Rocky said, "What's going on? What's going to happen?"

Hal looked at him curiously. Hal's face was a bright smear in the gloom of the booth. Near the projector, a half-eaten sandwich lay in white paper. A red light gave the room a sepulchral cast. Hal's hands hung at his sides like dead chickens. "Not sure."

Rocky looked for the *Snapshot* tins from Media Mass and saw the empty container of the one they just saw. "Is that it?"

"Far as I can tell, there's one more."

"I'm not sure I want to see it, but I think I have to. When would you show it?"

"I'd guess late next week." Hal smiled and Rocky saw that his teeth crossed in front, giving him an air of child-like absurdity. Hal played with a button with his long yellow fingers. "Kinda grabs you, don't it? It's kinda like we're watchin' something familiar about ourselves, but different, eerie."

Rocky shook hands again and felt the scrape of Hal's fingernails. Then he turned and walked down the stairs. The Markee was a dump, but it had a secure feel to it, eternal, as if the play of light and dark mirrored the play of life and death outside. It was ironic, Rocky thought. The Rex, the Markee...living on borrowed time, like everything else.

Rocky walked slowly out of the Markee. Outside, he blinked, adjusting his eyes to the glare of Forty-second Street. An old hotel, the Amsterdam, reared up west in the distance.

Rocky stuck his hands deep in his pockets and walked slowly over to Broadway. He didn't want to be alone that night. He took a bus downtown to the Village. Students, office workers, a few bums, a schizoid black man mixing a word salad brought back the tattered moviegoers in the Markee, *Snapshot*. They were vignettes, tiny moments tied incomprehensibly to life. The limo bulked heavily as one's vehicle in life. Speeding down a darkened tunnel, trying to see, but not seeing, imagining a bucolic life at the far end, dreaming. Could we find our dreams, or were we destined to crash? Was it original guilt, or local relative ones?

The Dew Drop Inn. Marley, the owner, was an old man, a nice man. The bar was old and couldn't compete with the newer fancier ones. Everyone's finances hung by a thread, but they paid rent and ate what they wanted. Life was good. He hiked the Sawtooth, walked the lava fields of the Craters of the Moon, got stuck in the snow. It was an easy time, a good time.

Despondent, reflective, Rocky walked slowly through happy Village crowds to Mariam's apartment building. He punched Mariam's number, then tapped his thick finger impatiently on the wooden door, waiting for her to buzz him in.

\* \* \*

"You have to choose your obsessions," said Mariam.

They were lying in bed staring at Mariam's ceiling. In back of them, on either side, barred windows let in weak light, barring the covers, and lighted the floor, a huge bronze vase of dried flowers, an old claw-legged oak table, and two hanging faux-Tiffany lamps. Beyond was a dim hallway hung on the door side with coats, dresses, and bags. Rocky felt he was inside a jewelry box.

"If we could identify obsessions, we wouldn't have them," said Rocky brusquely.

Mariam shrugged. "There are healthy obsessions and unhealthy ones. At least that's what I think; I'm just talking out loud. Sometimes you do that not knowing if what you're saying is true or not, or whether it matters."

Rocky rubbed his head, flattening his curls. "Stabs in dark," said Rocky. "I like that. We're never absolutely right, and most of the time we're close to dead wrong."

Mariam turned to look at him. "Where's *Snapshot* on that grid?"

The *Snapshot* trailers followed him up to Mariam's, through their lovemaking, touching, and rare cigarette. They hovered on the shifting line between explanation and path. Had those trailers become an obsession? Rocky didn't think so; they were a curiosity. If he tried hard, he could see them as a spiritual rise and fall of Rocky Morceau. Of course, they were so vague they could have been the rise and fall of anyone.

Rocky stared at one of Mariam's hats in the hallway, a flapper cap, which he couldn't remember she'd worn. "Why can't we stay innocent?"

"There's more to life than innocence. You've had a good life, no?"

Rocky frowned. "Ups and downs. Some bad times."

"Which you haven't told me about. You liked Boise, didn't you? The hiking, the Valley of the Moon. It sounds exotic and exciting."

Rocky said ruefully, "Yes, a good time."

Marian arranged the bed covers so they were neat and tucked around her legs like a mummy. "*Snapshot* reminds me of *Last Year at Marienbad*. Did you see it?"

Rocky rubbed his gray/white curls then said, "I've seen a lot of movies, especially after Claire died. But I didn't see that one. The Nouvelle Vague rolled right over Doc and me."

Mariam tilted her head up, as if she were picking out ideas swirling under the yellow ceiling. "Antonioni shot a serial movie, a mystery, but you were never sure of the crime. Then he cut up the scenes and mixed them randomly for the final cut."

Rocky moved slightly towards Mariam. On the wall, past her head, was a print of Kokoschka's dreaming princess isolated on her island. "That print is just like *Snapshot*. It's lonely, disorienting."

Mariam glanced at the print. "I bought it when I was alone. It represented how I felt. I should take it down now. As for *Snapshot*, maybe the point, like *Marienbad*, is that life is random, non-linear."

"It sure isn't *The Godfather* or *Bullitt*. The last clip showed a long tunnel with a flicker at the tunnel mouth. I couldn't make it out. That's worse, seeing something you should know, but not knowing what it is," said Rocky. "I don't want to see more but feel I have to."

"Maybe it's something we know but try to forget. It's about our inner demise. The director is showing you the final destruction of Willie's spirit."

"I wonder whether he committed suicide because he had notions of innocence and decay but no real theme."

"Like most of us," Mariam said. "How many of us start out in life and say that we're going to make our actions conform to themes?"

Mariam put her hand over his.

Rocky smiled at her. He felt the curve of her hip beneath the sheets. *Snapshot*. Was there a link between reality and the mock-up he saw in *Snapshot*? Or was it just about Rocky Morceau's need to see the link?

\* \* \*

Rocky left Mariam reluctantly. She had work, her boutique. Mariam said *Snapshot* was having an effect on him because he didn't have anything to do. He knew she was right. And she was right about not going to the Markee. He spent what seemed a long week walking, in long lunches,

135

at an opening in the East Village. The opening was a mistake; the red and black slashes of a Bacon imitator brought *Snapshot* right back. He came back to the Rex slightly drunk, his head full of images of skewed buildings and ominous shadows.

Thursday, he ate a desultory breakfast at the Odyssey. He stood outside the OTB for a few minutes. He watched bets made, bettors staring at the results, paper littering the floor.

He picked up the *Times* and a coffee and read the paper in his room. Reagan and Bush. More war. More atrocities. More corruption. No wonder we're compromised. Clinton might make it. Would he make it or succumb? He scanned the "Arts" section of the *Times*. Sappy chick flicks, dopey comedies. Big-budget high-tech blood-and-guts and smash-'em-ups were strewn garishly over pages after page.

*Brrring, brrring.*

Rocky stared at the phone as if he knew it was going to be bad news. He lifted the receiver. Hal. The Markee was showing a Sergio Leone marathon and afterwards the last *Snapshot* trailer.

Rocky thanked him. He paced his room. Finally he robotically put on his heavy coat and gloves and headed for the Circle, a twenty-four-hour diner near Fourteenth Street. After lunch, he walked briskly in the cold to Times Square.

He paid his two bucks to Leon and found his favorite seat on the left of the screen, halfway down. He didn't have to worry it was taken. The place seated a thousand, and there were barely twenty—the same ten homeless lumps spread over the back row and a few guys like him scattered through the house.

He sat through the spaghetti westerns, the Sergio Leone spatter-fests starring the man with no name, who, of course, had a very well-known name, Clint Eastwood. There was Clint squinting into the sun, chomping on a thin black cigar, sizing up his opponents, whipping back his huarache, letting his gun flick out like a metal snake. Rocky let the desert sand wash over him and frame the unstoppable force, the im-movable obstacle.

At six, recess was over. His eyes were about to roll down the aisle. He felt a rush of blood, an edgy anticipation.

The screen flickered. A long tracking shot of *Snapshot* rolled over the screen. No synopsis that time. Huge black limo accelerating, tires screeching down a dark road lined with trees.

Then it was as if that mad Polish director had forgotten what he was doing. Country scene full of tinkling music, farm animals, bright green fields, a rustic red barn, a white church, its steeple piercing the blue sky. Then a rotating tire and the black limo windows half-open, white smear of faces. It roared down a tunnel; the distant tunnel mouth was a half-circle of light, a small flame. The noise of screeching tires reverberated off the walls.

Then the camera careened like a bronco. Rocky got dizzy, disoriented. He gripped the arms of the chair. Then there were slow outtakes of a limo parked in a garage, a distant scream, a flash of light, as if a match had been lit, then extinguished.

Tunnel, shadowy alley. Two men pounded an inert figure, their fists rising and falling metronomically. He couldn't see what, or who, was being beaten.

The screen filled with a potlatch of violence. Decapitations, dismemberment, flaying, blood everywhere, a charnel house. The last scene was Willie surrounded by bloody bent bodies crouching over a man, rifling his pockets. Willie looked up, the man's wallet in his bloody hand. Willie's tiny red eyes stared straight at him, and Rocky felt the hairs on his neck rise, his scalp tingle. Willie's expression was beyond malevolent. It was a dare; it grabbed into the roots of his consciousness. Rocky's fingers ground into the frayed arms of the seat.

*Snapshot* faded; the theatre darkened, lightened. He was alone in the theatre. Trembling, he got up and shuffled towards the exit. He glanced at the stairway up to the projection booth but shook his head no.

* * *

*Snapshot* wormed its way through his brain. Flashes everywhere. Jerky shadows. Willie stared at him from the mirror. What had he become? He had no job, no money, no prospects. What made him become what he was? Was it the rootless existence with Claire and Doc? Was it his failing ability to prove himself? How can he find out? He couldn't live as a failure. He had dreams. He had joyous times before him; he wasn't spent, a thief.

The faces of the Rex tenants accused him. His floor was dark, skewed, as if it had changed overnight into a place remote and mysterious. Small sounds, a rapping on a door, the scruff of shoes over the carpet.

Mariam called him Friday morning. She wanted to get out of the city.

She said, "It will be a holiday."

He felt he was riding on the edge of sanity, but finally he said it was okay; it would be good. He supposed it would be good out of his room, the floor, the Rex. The country, even in winter, would be an escape.

Friday, late, Rocky walked slowly over to Midtown to pick up the rental. When he saw the car, he asked for another. It was a pitch-black Toyota.

"Don't you have any others?"

"That's it, Mac. Everything else is reserved."

Mariam was in a bubbly mood, glad they could get away. He tried to feel that way; he liked to get away, to break the routines. But he felt different, as if a switch had been thrown. He tried to analyze it but failed. It was Willie; it was looking in the mirror and seeing Willie. Willie and the director died unredeemed. He would too.

The West Side Highway was crowded, and it took a long time to get to the George Washington Bridge. On the bridge, he tried to lighten up.

"We haven't been upstate for a month. It feels good to get away."

Mariam smiled. "You say that as if you meant it."

"What does that mean?" Rocky said angrily.

"You're distracted, somewhere else. If I were to guess, your head is full of those stupid trailers. Some movies stay with you; *Snapshot* isn't even a movie."

Rocky gripped the wheel, shook his head. "It was too close, you know."

"You've been talking about it for weeks. When we get upstate we should talk it out. It would be good for both of us."

"I don't know if I want to talk about it at all."

The traffic on the Palisades Parkway was light.

There was a turn in the road. A bright light flashed down a tunnel of trees. The darkness hemmed him in. He squinted, trying to see the light. Sweat dripped down his neck. He felt he was slowing down, the traffic backing up. A black Mercedes veered around him. A face smeared across the window leered at him. Marley!

"No!"

Rocky braked and, tires squealing, swerved into a gas station. The car rocked to a stop, askew, headlights pointed towards the opposite lane of the parkway. Light from traffic grew on the backs of cars at the pump and faded.

Snowflakes drifted down, hit the windshield, disappeared. It seemed uncommonly peaceful, as if time had stopped. If only they could stay like that, unmoving, stopped, not going forward or back. But that wasn't the way.

Rocky shook his head sadly. His story came out in a tumble of words about the bar, stealing from Marley, the OTB, Marley losing the bar, Marley's suicide. As he talked, the grip on his mind loosened. His face relaxed as if it had been pulled back tight for days.

He felt a hand in his hair. He rested his head on Mariam's shoulder.

Rocky said, "I wish I could take it back, or see that old man again."

"Marley can't forgive you. But I will."

Rocky let out his breath slowly into Mariam's neck.

# Coda

They call it April Fool's Day in America. People run around and play tricks on their friends and neighbors. Some fun.

Rudi shook his head and wondered about his adopted country; it saved him, it held out a hand to him, but America trivialized everything! He wasn't sure how they did it. They made love, life, death, a way to sell something; they made it insignificant. That was the only way he could think of describing it—insignificant!

It was a slow day, and Rudi closed the ledger, propped his glasses in his hair, and came out from around the desk hoping the phone wouldn't ring for a few minutes. Even if it did, he didn't care if he missed a call—if it was important, they'd call back. Since Gino died, Rudi had become semi-permanent daytime flak-catcher at the desk, but fortunately (unfortunately, if you were Bill) Bill was laid off his other job, worked more with the band-aids, and did the desk at night.

The front door was open; it was a nice spring day, middle of the afternoon. Slow, very slow. Rudi walked out the open door and down the worn, shallow steps. He glanced up at the torn canopy and shook his head. He'd put tape on it last fall, and it had already come off. Band-aid, band-aid. That's all he could do.

Rudi walked past the Moat, turned, and looked back at the Rex.

He saw it every day when he came to work, and every day when he left to catch the subway at Twenty-eighth Street, he looked at it again, worried about how strong it was, or whether it was going to start disintegrating in front of his eyes, stone by stone, window by window, until it was down to the foundation, like a collapsible building. Rudi knew it was solid, but he had a feeling it wasn't solid enough; it could develop a little crack... that would become a big crack, a hole where the rain and wind and snow would sweep in. Sometimes he had an idea that some force outside was waiting for a small crack, and then it was over.

Rudi had to admire the people. They had their little cracks—some, big cracks—but they didn't give up. And that's what made him feel Ben was wrong. The people in the Rex were the best argument against Ben.

They lived in an impossible neighborhood, surrounded by new fatuous wealth, arrogant people who spent more on their fancy dogs than rent for a year at the Rex, and they didn't give up. They made their adjustments, they survived, and that gave Rudi hope. Inside, outside: they were both old, both frayed, and a few more of those inside had unraveled, but he had hope for both of them.

If he had only the physical building and residents to worry about...

It happened every spring: a wealthy developer or landlord would drive past and see the shabby side of the Rex—not the solid side Rudi saw—and compare it to the buildings around it and know it was a gold mine no one else had seen. It didn't take a genius, thought Rudi. They all thought they were geniuses, and all they had was money, greed, and a stale idea about another high-rise. Rudi never liked Michael Mitchell. He wanted the Rex in the worst way. Two of Rudi's partners wanted it: the Rex wasn't a great proposition—they made a little money, but it wasn't worth the repairs, the constant worry a catastrophe would wipe out their small profit and they'd have to spend thousands to keep the Rex running. It could be anything; the boiler was held together with paste, the plumbing, the electric, the elevator—the elevator!—a fire inspection, asbestos—who knew what problems were hidden in the ancient walls of the Rex?

It was very close, and Mitchell wasn't happy. His eyes had devoured the Rex, his checkbook was on the table, pen out; it was drama, and they were close to going for it. Mitchell was part of the problem; he was short and fat—a little like Gino. But Rudi would have preferred Gino any day, may he rest in peace. Mitchell sweated an oil of greed that soaked the office. He'd taken the big chair, his feet were on the desk, and he put his fat finger on the yellow wall as if he were seeing how long it would take to come down—as if he already owned it! In the end his partners reacted the way he did, and dislike of Mitchell and conservatism won. It wasn't just Mitchell; his partners knew the Rex, its problems, how much they could expect from it, and they didn't know much else. They had larger shares than he did, but if they sold the Rex, most of them wouldn't own anything. They'd have no income; they wouldn't know where to put their money. In the back of their minds, they knew they could figure that out, but they went with what they knew. They could count on the Rex.

They won that round, but Rudi knew—knew!—Mitchell would be back, and if not Mitchell, someone equally greedy. It was a matter of time.

www.ingramcontent.com/pod-product-compliance
Lightning Source LLC
Chambersburg PA
CBHW030619130626
46552CB00002B/640